RUNAWAY **BEST SELLER**

a novel

L E E   S I L B E R

ALSO BY LEE SILBER

RUNAWAY **BEST SELLER**

a novel

L E E   S I L B E R

Published by Deep Impact Publishing

822 Redondo Court

San Diego CA 92109

To buy copies of this book in bulk, inquire about a presentation based on this story, or get a free copy of the companion guide featuring photographs of the places featured in the book, please contact the author at:
www.leesilber.com, 858-735-4533, leesilber@leesilber.com

Cover and Interior Design: Lee Silber

Layout and Typesetting: Andrew Chapman

First Print Edition January 2013

Retail Price: $11.00

This book is dedicated to my wife, Andrea, who believed me when I said someday I would write a "runaway best seller."

PROLOGUE

Angel arrived home and dropped his garment bag on the marble floor just inside the front doors of his estate, staring at the scene in front of him. He reached down and picked up one of the hundreds of pieces of paper strewn all over the normally neat house. In an instant he realized. Kate knew about the affair. He felt a twinge of remorse, but that was quickly replaced by rage and the familiar burning behind his eyes. The anger boiling up from his belly.

"KATE!" Angel searched through the house, picking up papers and scanning them along the way. "Kate, you nosey little bitch. You'll pay for this, I swear to God."

After searching the entire downstairs Angel found Kate standing at the top of the wide staircase, glaring at him.

"How could you?" She screamed. "How could you do this to me?" Kate clutched one of the printouts.

Angel climbed the stairs, arms outstretched in a sign of surrender, "Baby, I'm sorry. I wasn't thinking. She meant nothing to me. You know I love you."

As Angel approached Kate backed away, her elbows tight against her sides, and her hands covered her mouth. She was looking down at the paper that fell from her hand. "Who is she?" Kate flung the piece of paper at Angel.

Angel glanced at the print out. It was one of many explicit e-mails sent to him from a woman named Teri. This time it wouldn't be so easy to explain away his extracurricular activities since the proof was right there in black and white.

Angel pounced, grabbed her by the arms and shook her hard. "You fucking worthless whore. How dare you read my e-mail. I'll kill you!" Angel punched her in the chest. The blow seemed to take her breath away. Kate fell to the ground and gasped for air. Angel grabbed her hair, swung her around and dragged her down the stairs. When she reached up and tried to hold onto Angel's arm to take the pressure off her scalp, he pulled even harder. Angel screamed and threw her in a heap on the floor at the base of the stairs.

"I'm going to teach you a lesson you will not soon forget, you bitch. You do not snoop around in other people's private things," and he kicked her hard in the side.

Kate wailed in pain and curled up on the floor. "I'm sorry. I'm sorry. I'm sorry."

"You better be, bitch." Angel pulled her up by her hair. Angel felt an uncontrollable rage take control of him and he continued his diatribe. "What I do when I'm on the road is my business, so stay out of it. Got it? Can you do that? Is that too much to ask?"

Angel felt Kate try to nod, but it was impossible with him yanking her hair.

"I give you everything you want. Do you know how many women want to be married to a guy like me?" Angel looked down at his beaten wife. She said nothing. "I'll tell you. A lot. You don't have to work. You don't have to clean. You barely cook. All you have to do is be a good little wife. Then you go and do this." He threw one of the printouts in her face. "You are an ungrateful bitch, you know that?"

He spit on her and continued screaming, only now in Spanish. Angel often wondered if Kate had secretly mastered the language, but he doubted it and spoke freely around her with his family and friends—many times saying things he didn't want her to hear. Now he hoped she did understand, because he used every curse word he knew in his native tongue. It was almost as if he was scolding a small child, but instead of spanking, he punched her in the face and Kate dropped to the floor.

"You better hope I didn't hurt my hand," Angel said and rubbed his knuckles.

Kate cowered and covered her left eye. She was on her knees and seemed to waiting for the next blow but he didn't hit her again, temporarily preoccupied with his hand. Kate crawled on her hands and knees and scooped up the love letters. If this was her attempt at cleaning up to appease him, it wouldn't work. He was pissed.

"Now look what you've done. You got blood all over my favorite shirt," he said.

The last thing Kate would see before her world went black was Angel's boot heading hard and fast for her head.

CHAPTER 1

Angel looked at his lawyer, then turned to two the detectives. "I didn't kill my wife," he said with a curious calm.

"Why would anyone believe you, Angel? Because you play professional baseball? I'm not a big fan of the sport. How about you, Detective Lambert?" Detective Morrison knew the answer his partner was going to give.

"Nah, I'm not into it, either. Too slow for me. Besides, it's not like baseball players are real athletes, anyway," Lambert said, trying to goad Angel. It was no secret he had a propensity to fly off the handle, and possibly say something he didn't mean, when in an agitated state. "Baseball is boring. And Angel, you don't really look like an athlete anyway. You look out of shape to me. I prefer my men lean and mean and you only possess one of those two characteristics."

Angel mumbled something in Spanish, looking to his lawyer for help.

"Do you have a question for my client? We'd like to get this cleared up as quickly as possible so he can get to the ballpark in time for tonight's game." Angel's attorney checked his watch. He appeared oblivious to the seriousness of the situation.

"Well, counselor, that's just not gonna happen," Detective Morrison said. "Not tonight, not any night. His playing days are over. Oh, he'll be catching again, just not for the Padres. He'll be catching some longing glances from the other inmates in prison, because that's where he's going."

"A guy like you, Angel, well, you're going to find out what it's like to be an abused woman once you're incarcerated." Detective Lambert placed her hands on the table, encroaching on Angel's personal space.

"I can't believe this. I told you, I didn't kill my wife." Angel confidently leaned back in his chair as he said this.

"Okay, we're done here. Either charge my client or let him go," Angel's attorney said, sounding a little less than convincing.

"Before we place him under arrest, we'd like to give your client a chance to come clean and shave some years off his sentence. Premeditated murder goes into extra innings, if you know what I mean," Morrison said.

The attorney waved his hand dismissively before saying, "No, I don't think so. We're —"

"Angel," Morrison interrupted, "let us give you the play-by-play of what we believe happened to your wife. If at any time you want to call time out and confess, feel free to do so."

Angel and his lawyer slumped back down. Detective Lambert turned the page on the flip chart in the corner of the room. In big block letters the word *Means* was written on the first page. "It seems that our boy, Angel here, is quite a hitter, and I don't mean at the plate. He likes to strike women."

Morrison threw a manila folder on the table and opened it. "Says here, Angel, you were cited several times for assault and battery in your youth—two against girls. Then there are the fights outside bars and inside strip clubs—one of which resulted in felony charges and civil action. You have some anger management issues."

Angel looked at the wall while his attorney ran his finger down the rap sheet. Angel knew he was seeing these charges for the first time, since he had never mentioned them before. His attorney glanced at him, then read the long list of offenses—all of them either dropped, pleaded down to community service, or involved probation, except for one incident where Angel assaulted an off-duty police officer during his rookie year in the league. That one didn't go away so easily. Angel had pleaded no contest and was sentenced to house arrest for 90 days, and he'd paid off the officer to prevent the details from becoming public.

"Then there's the three D.U.I.s. You don't learn from your mistakes, do you, Angel?" Morrison continued while Lambert paced the room, tapping a folder.

Angel didn't answer. He drove drunk almost every night. It was a miracle he only got caught three times.

"I read somewhere that you're being investigated by Major League Baseball for using steroids to prolong your career," Lambert said. "Hey, Morrison, don't steroids make most people more violent?"

"That's what I hear. They can't control their rage. Is that what happened, Angel? You went into a steroid-fueled rage and couldn't stop yourself?"

He didn't say a word. He'd been using steroids since the 1997 season when the aches and pains of over 1,000 games crouched behind the plate were catching up to him. The steroids did help his performance on the field and in bed, but they also made it impossible for him to control his temper.

"You're not denying that you used steroids. Using illegal drugs may not be that big a deal, but these charges, Angel, are serious, don't you think?" Detective Morrison pointed to another page in the thick file. "It says here that you battered your girlfriend in San Francisco four years ago. When were you and Kate married, Angel?" Morrison said.

Angel mumbled, "2000."

"So, five years ago. Is that right?" Morrison asked.

Angel nodded.

"Did Kate know you had a girlfriend when you played for the Giants? Just after the two of you were married?"

Lambert interjected, "Just so you know, I'm not a big fan of men who cheat and beat their significant others."

Angel shrugged.

"How about this one, Angel?" Detective Morrison pointed to another page in the folder. "You hit a woman in Toronto while playing for the Blue Jays. You got her pregnant and proceeded to batter her even after she was carrying your baby."

Angel was surprised that this information was out there. His attorney shook his head, then sat back, with arms crossed.

"Didn't think we could find out about crimes committed in Canada, did you, Angel?" Morrison asked.

The detectives didn't miss the fact that Angel's attorney was quickly losing his interest in defending someone who had a track record of violence—domestic and otherwise and exchanged a satisfied grin.

"Hey Angel, it looks like you hit for the cycle here." Lambert flipped a page. "The police have come to your home on, let me see here... one, two, three, four, five different occasions for complaints about domestic abuse by one Katherine Ramirez. Your wife may have dropped the charges every time, but we have the 9-1-1 tapes, if you'd like to hear them." This wasn't true, since those calls would've been erased by this point, but they knew Angel wouldn't know that.

Morrison snapped another folder down on the table and opened it to reveal photos of Kate with a black eye, welts, and various other injuries. "We found this in your wife's nightstand. Guess she had a friend take 'em for safekeeping. Juries love photos like these." The detective smiled and flipped the photos over one by one for Angel and his attorney to see.

Angel glanced at his attorney, who by now had the same look of a starting pitcher who was finished for the day and needed a reliever to come in and save the game. Angel could only guess the photos were too much for a guy who specialized in sports law and didn't deal with criminal matters. He needed one more inning from his lawyer because there wasn't anyone warming up in the bullpen.

"Angel? What have you got to say for yourself?"

Morrison asked.

Angel tried to keep the smirk from his face when he lingered a little too long looking at the photos of his battered wife, then turned to his attorney for support, but none was forthcoming. "Okay, I have trouble controlling my emotions. I admit it. I'll get some counseling. But I'm telling you guys, I did not kill my wife." Angel expected that this admission and act of contrition would resolve the entire issue once and for all.

"Hey, I'm sensing a deal coming on," Morrison said. "We can trade murder for manslaughter, if that's your defense, Angel. What do you think, counselor? Man-two with a sentencing recommendation for an admission of guilt under emotional duress?"

"I'm not pleading to anything," Angel said on behalf of himself and his mute attorney.

"Well, it's still early in the game, Angel, so let's see what's up next." Lambert flipped the page over on the easel to reveal another word written in bold ink on the big pad of paper: *Motive*. "We found over a hundred copies of the love letters your wife printed out from your email inbox."

Angel rolled his eyes.

"You really should take out the trash more often. So, your wife caught you cheating on her again, only this time she had you by the balls. She was going to divorce you and take half of everything you own," Lambert said. "That's motive, in case you're keeping score."

Angel glanced at his lawyer who was still transfixed on the photos of a beaten Kate. "Aren't you going to object or say something?" the ballplayer said, his voice a bit more agitated than it had been so far.

"Uh, enough with the clever baseball metaphors, detectives, okay?"

"That's it?" Angel replied as he gave his attorney the evil eye.

The attorney just glanced back at him. Angel then whispered into his attorney's ear for nearly a minute. This seemed to snap the counselor out of his inaction and he slipped back into lawyer mode. "Yes, my client has a violent past. Yes, he has cheated on his wife. Yes, he got caught. But I still see no evidence that he killed his wife or that she's even dead."

Angel straightened his shoulders and raised his chin, a smile spreading across his face. More confident now, he spoke in his own defense. "There is no way Kate was going to divorce me. No way."

"Oh, really, and why is that?" Lambert asked. Angel said nothing. "Because you killed her, right? Dead wives don't get anything in a divorce settlement, do they, counselor?"

"I still see no evidence of a murder here, detectives," Angel's lawyer said.

"Let's not get ahead of ourselves. First, let's recap. Your client had the means and the motive to kill his wife. That much we've already established. How about opportunity?" Morrison turned the page on the easel to reveal the word *Opportunity* in block letters.

"What do you mean?" Angel asked.

"Where were you the night of August 10th?" Detective Morrison inquired as he reached for yet another folder.

"I dunno."

"Well, according to this Padres schedule you returned from a road trip to the east coast that same day and played the Reds in San Diego that night," Morrison said without looking up from his notes.

"Says here you went hitless that night—at least in the game. Too bad," Lambert added.

"Yeah, I remember that game. What's-his-name started for the Reds."

"Paul Wilson," Morrison said.

"So, you were in town. Did you go home after the game?" Lambert asked.

"I dunno."

"What's your point?" Angel's attorney said.

"Well, it says here, counselor, your boy got a parking ticket in La Jolla early in the morning on August 11th. We canvassed the neighborhood and it turns out that Angel spent the night at a woman's condo. Jody Bennington, 4380 La Jolla Village Drive. In fact, she's told us you stayed there the entire few days until your next road trip."

"So?" The attorney spoke on behalf of Angel, who was surprised the police were this thorough.

Detective Morrison looked up and said, "You still live at 457 Blue Anchor Road in Coronado, don't you, Angel?"

"Proving?" The attorney asked before Angel could answer.

"Now, this is just a theory, but let's just say Angel killed Kate that morning during a heated argument, disposed of the body before the game, and afterwards went to his girlfriend's house to celebrate his newfound freedom," Detective Morrison said.

Angel shot up from his chair. "That's not true! Yeah, I got back from Houston that morning. I was in a slump and sore and tired and when I came home Kate had all these goddamn papers all over the floor." Angel held up one of the printouts in a clear evidence bag.

"Look, guys, you've got a lot of circumstantial theories, but no evidence of a murder. Come on Angel, we're leaving." The attorney stood.

"Just a minute. We were saving the best for last. See this, Angel?" Morrison held up another manila folder. "It's a report from forensics. Guess what it says we found in your home when the crime scene team went through there?"

Angel was silent.

"You're both gonna want to sit down for this."

Angel and his attorney reluctantly sat back down. Another folder joined the pile.

"Let me just give you the highlights. Kind of like a *Sports Center* version of the evidence."

Angel's attorney groaned. Another sports metaphor.

"Let's see, blood splatters on the wall at the top of the stairway and in the living room. Oh, our tests revealed they belonged to one Katherine Ramirez," Morrison said. "Then there is a broken fingernail that also belonged to her, with a good amount of skin under it. I wonder if that skin will prove to be yours, Angel?"

"Don't forget the partial shoeprint in that one blood spot," Lambert interjected. "I'll bet that matches one of Angel's shoes."

"What your tests don't say, and can't say, is *when* those bloodstains got there," replied the attorney. "And a broken fingernail? Really?"

"The tests may not tell us, but the maids can. See, these weren't small stains, counselor. They were fairly large. See for yourself," Lambert said as she waited expectantly for the lawyer's reaction.

Detective Morrison leaned forward and produced a stack of photos. "The maid service wouldn't have missed these and, in fact, they didn't. See, those stains were not there the last time the maids cleaned the Ramirez's residence on August 9th, as their affidavit clearly states. That was just the day before. The next time, a week later during their regularly scheduled visit, they came upon the horrible crime scene, when they called us to report what they found. So, we've narrowed our time frame a bit, don't you think?"

Angel stood up as if to leave. "Anyone could have broken into our home while I was away and killed my wife. Anyone. What is with you cops? You jealous that a Latino like me can make so much money while you get your government pay?"

"So then," Morrison said calmly, "why did you not go home all that week? Why did you not report your wife missing?"

"You know," Angel answered with a look.

"Yeah, you were at your girlfriend's and then you were on the road. But then why did you not report Kate missing?"

"What? I was gone. You said so yourself. I didn't know where Kate was."

"But we've got your cell phone records, Angel. Why would a jealous, possessive man like you just go away for a week and not call her? There's not a single call to her phone. I find that very curious."

"I don't know. Maybe I just wanted to leave her be, you know, let her cool down a bit after what happened."

"Yeah, Morrison replied, "let her get nice and cold at the bottom of the ocean where you dumped her." Morrison then nodded at Detective Lambert and said, "Do you want to tell them or should I?"

"Naw, you tell them." Lambert smiled.

"While you were on the road, Angel, we had some time to ourselves, some time to dig into things—literally."

"Yeah, so?"

Officer Morrison produced another evidence bag, this one containing a mint-green silk dress shirt. "Found this buried under the bushes by your driveway," he said. "Bad job burying it, I might add. You'd think a catcher would do a better job of getting down into the dirt."

Angel said nothing, but Lambert could see his nostrils flaring as he started to breathe more heavily. She decided to add a little more info. "Two of your teammates will testify that they saw you wearing this very same shirt on the team's charter flight back from Houston the morning of the 10th. Guess what's on it, Angel?"

Again, Angel didn't say a word.

"Blood," Morrison said. "Kate's blood."

"This is all bullshit!" Angel suddenly belted out, rising from his chair as quickly as he would to stop a wild pitch. "You guys are full of shit. She's alive somewhere, and you're just trying to pin this on me! Stick it to the Latino, right?" Angel's eyes were on fire. His chest heaved with each breath as he stopped ranting to regain his composure. Lambert and Morrison remained calm, unfazed by the outburst they had been hoping for. They turned their attention to the attorney.

"Counselor," Morrison said, "we'll share a few more facts with you, which might help in talking some sense into your client. One, we have video from the security cameras at the Ramirez household showing Angel hauling a large duffel bag to his car not long after he killed Kate—corroborated by a neighbor who witnessed the same. Two, we have multiple areas of blood evidence on your client's boat—looks like he cleaned it up pretty good, but not good enough. Three, a boater reported to the Coast Guard seeing another boater dumping what was described as, and I quote, "a large, heavy bag" in the ocean off Point Loma on the 10th. The suspect boat matches your client's boat, and the timing would be perfect with the time it would have taken Angel to get out there from his home."

"This is fucked," Angel said, shaking his head in disbelief. "I didn't dump anything in the ocean. I didn't even go out on my boat that day. The duffel bag was the one I took to my... to Jody's place."

"Yeah, well it's only a matter of time before the Coast Guard turns up that bag or it washes ashore."

Morrison then gestured to Lambert, who placed a small digital recorder on the table. With a click of the button, Kate's voice came out loud and clear: "You know, one day I'm not going to put up with this anymore. One day I will finally leave and take everything you own!"

Then Angel was heard on the recording, in an ominously calm tone: "You might want to think before you do that, because I will kill you. You hear me? You will be dead in a ditch in Tijuana before you ever get a thing from me." Lambert clicked the recorder off.

"You didn't know she'd recorded that conversation, Angel, did you?"

Angel started to say something, but his attorney put his hand across his chest to indicate it was time to stop talking. He then whispered something to Angel. Angel whispered back and the lawyer cleared his throat. "Angel admits that he and his wife got into an argument and that he may have hit her, but it was in self-defense. She was the one who attacked him."

"Really. So what you're saying then, Angel, is your wife, who is..." Detective Morrison checked her driver's license information before finishing, "5 feet 4 inches tall and weighs 118 pounds, attacked you and you were merely defending yourself?"

"Yeah, that's right."

Morrison turned to Lambert and quietly said, "I guess I should say Kate *was* 5 feet 4 since—"

"Like I said," Angel interjected, "I didn't kill her!"

Morrison ignored him, attempting to piss him off just a bit more. "And you're what, 6 foot 3? Weigh about 220 pounds? Am I right?"

Angel said nothing nor did his attorney.

Morrison continued. "You were the one being attacked? I mean, come on, Angel. Puleeze. Your wife was clearly brutally attacked by a man much larger than her."

"How do you know that?" asked the attorney.

"Take a look at this," Morrison said, dropping another clear evidence bag on the table in front of Angel's attorney.

"What's this?" the lawyer said before looking at the contents.

"That, counselor, is a piece of your client's wife's scalp," said Lambert.

The attorney stared at the small flap of skin with long dark hairs coming out of it. Wincing, he pushed the bag across the table.

Morrison continued: "We also have fragments of teeth, if you're interested in seeing those."

Angel held back a smirk. Ignoring the bloody, fleshy evidence, he said, "I already told you, I didn't kill my wife. I admit I may have had to hit her to calm her down, but I didn't kill her."

"You didn't *mean* to kill her," Morrison said. "Isn't that right? We're open to your story there, Angel, but it's got to be 100% truth. Don't keep giving us this line that you didn't kill her. We know you did. But you know what? I don't think you meant to. I think it was just a tired man who'd gotten home from a long trip, got some news he didn't like, and things got out of control. Isn't that what we're talking about here?"

Detective Lambert had moved to a spot right next to Angel. She bent down and said quietly in his ear, "My partner might think you have an excuse, but I don't. I know you killed her on purpose, and I'm going to make sure everyone knows." Lambert stood back up and looked to Angel for a response, but he sat motionless, never even glancing up at her.

"Angel, don't say another word. Is my client under arrest?" the attorney asked.

Lambert looked to Morrison, who backed off his line of questioning for the time being. He knew there'd be another crack at Angel. All they needed now was the confession, and it was probably time to let Angel sit tight with the idea of pleading to an assault that just went too far. If that didn't work, they could always hang the death penalty over his head as a prospect.

"What do you think?" said Lambert. "It's three strikes and you're out, right, Angel?"

Angel ignored her.

"For the record, my client vehemently denies he murdered his wife."

"Duly noted, counselor," she acknowledged. "But let me ask Angel one last question before I place him under arrest for murder." She sat in the chair directly across from the ballplayer, to make solid eye contact. "Where is your wife? She hasn't been seen or heard from since the day you admit to beating the living crap out of her. Hell, all her credit cards, her driver's license, her cell phone, everything—it was all left at your house. She didn't even take the $235 in cash in her purse. Her SUV's not gone, and she didn't buy a bus, train, or plane ticket anywhere. She didn't rent a car anywhere. That's pretty incredible. But maybe she just flew to the moon. Really, Angel… if you didn't kill her, where is she?"

The attorney looked at Angel, who was suddenly looking very tired and could only say, "I don't know. I honestly don't know."

Detective Morrison began handcuffing Angel

while Detective Lambert began reading him his rights. "Angel Ramirez, you are under arrest for…"

CHAPTER 2

Kate took a deep breath of the tropical air and sped through the sugarcane fields in her bright red Jeep. She'd done it. She was free. The feeling of being on her own was intoxicating. She couldn't stop smiling. She took off her ball cap and looked in the rearview mirror and ran her hand through her now-short blond hair. She was a new person. The plastic surgeon in Los Angeles had done a phenomenal job with her scalp, not to mention the cuts and bruises that had marred her face. She had always held a distain for those shady Beverly Hills docs who did anything for their famous clients for the right amount of cash, but she had to admit it made her escape possible. The doc even threw in a few cosmetic changes that would make her less recognizable, even though she would be far from home. But most importantly, she now felt like a new person on the inside.

Now pulled over to the side of the road, Kate picked up the map of Kauai and glanced again at the highlighted path to her destination. The map wasn't really necessary on an island with only a handful of main roads, but she wanted to be sure she didn't have to stop and ask for directions and draw undue attention to herself. Sure, she looked like just another tourist, but the paranoia was real and being on the run would be a whole lot easier once she reached the remote side of the island and settled in.

Years of being beaten and abused by Angel, along with constant threats that if she ever left him he would hunt her down and kill her, made her cautious—for good reason. It would probably be years before she would be able to trust another man, let alone have a relationship.

She put the map back and glanced down at the brochure for the secluded hotel she had chosen to begin her new life. She had spent months preparing for her eventual escape, planning every step from her first day away from the mainland through the first three months. Of course, she hadn't planned on her path unfolding quite like it did—being badly beaten and having to spend time recovering in Los Angeles—but the best things in life usually come when preparation meets opportunity. And when that happens, things often fall right into place. How else to explain a driveable car popping up on Craigslist for $1,200 right when she needed to get away? Okay, so maybe it was stolen, considering the guy didn't have the title and didn't even ask about her clearly suspicious appearance, but it got her where she needed to go for a couple weeks. It got her to the boat she and Angel owned, where she'd stashed all her escape cash; it got her to L.A., where she was able to see Dr. Shabazi and recover in the hotel his brother owned; and it got her to LAX, where she was able to buy a first-class ticket courtesy of the false documentation she'd bought several weeks earlier.

The squawk of a bird overhead brought her back

to the moment. She put the Jeep in gear and pulled back onto the road. The fresh air blew all around her as she hummed along to the Hawaiian music on the radio. It was the first time she could ever remember when the reality was even better than the dream. The sun warming her face, the fragrance of the flowers, the soothing sounds of a Hawaiian ukelele, the lushness all around her were better than she ever could have imagined. She knew the name of every beach and small town along the way to her destination—the Plantation Inn.

The Inn was a favorite destination for famous writers who needed the seclusion to work on their books. Just past the town of Waimea, a speed bump of a place, really, the Inn had been a failed attempt by a wealthy plantation owner to convert a part of his property into a resort. After years of neglect, the cottages were remodeled and the Inn restored to its original luster. It sat in the middle of nowhere, and that's exactly why famous and ordinary people picked it as the perfect place to get away from it all.

The hotel respected people's privacy and didn't require a real name upon check-in, or the need for guests to secure their rooms with a credit card—cash would do. Kate had done enough research to know the Inn was rarely filled to capacity and very few tourists stopped by, except the occasional couple that needed a drink and a bite to eat after a long day at a secluded beach a dozen miles down the road.

※ ※ ※

Kate turned off the main road and headed for Salt Pond Beach Park. She slipped off her sun dress, glad to have worn a bikini, grabbed a towel, and headed across the grass to the beach. She jumped in the warm, salty water and floated. She felt all the pain and suffering from the past just melt away. Floating along the calm protected water a few feet from shore, she admired the azure blue of the cloudless sky and she began to cry.

She wasn't sure why the tears came. It was partly because she had allowed herself to be abused for so long and did nothing. She could have lived a life like this, years ago. Instead, she'd stayed with Angel, in part because she believed what she owned and the status of being married to a baseball player was important. That seemed so silly now. This is where she'd belonged all along.

She realized she was crying because she was free. Free to be what she always knew she should be, living a simple life on a tropical island. She wouldn't miss the big house, exotic cars or trendy clothes. Sure, she got some joy from decorating their home, shopping during the day in a car filled with the smell of fine Italian leather. But those things didn't make her happy. Not like she was at this moment.

※ ※ ※

Kate lingered under the park's outdoor shower a little longer than necessary. She simply wanted this feeling to last forever. Making her way to her Jeep, she saw a man with a van waving her over. Fear gripped her before she realized what he wanted. He had a handmade sign that read, *Puppies For Sale*.

"Aloha," he said.

"Aloha. What beautiful puppies," Kate said as one of the pups licked her hand. "What type of dogs are these?"

"Golden Labs. Great for the islands, yeah," the local man said in perfect pidgin. "The wife says I gotta get rid of half da litter. Too many mouths to feed already, yeah?"

Kate grinned at the Hawaiian man who smiled back, his yellow teeth glowing in the late afternoon sun. He looked like he could use the money. He wore red trunks and a well-worn t-shirt with the sleeves torn off and a pair of old flip-flops. His truck was so rusted it appeared as if it would just crumble into a pile of red sand.

"It looks like dis little guy likes you." The man held up one of the pups.

"I don't think I can keep a dog where I'm going," Kate said, but petted the puppy.

"Where you staying?"

"Uh, I just got here," Kate said, evading the question.

"Welcome to Kauai. My name is Kimo. I've lived on this side of the island my whole life. So where you gonna go?" Kimo asked.

Kate paused. Her intuition told her this man meant her no harm. "I'm on my way to the Plantation Inn."

Kimo smiled. "That's a good choice. Real quiet. My niece works at the front desk. She'll let you keep a dog. They keep it local style there." Kimo handed her the puppy to hold.

She felt the warmth and love from the puppy. He licked her face and neck. She glanced at Kimo. He smiled like a proud papa. "I don't know," she said. "I'm not sure I'm ready for that kind of commitment."

"I'll tell you what. Stop by here tomorrow and I'll save dis little guy in case you change your mind." Kimo took the puppy back.

"Okay, thanks."

"No problem. I'll call Vina and tell her to take good care of you." Kimo surprised her by pulling out a cell phone. "What's your name?"

"Really, you don't need to do that."

"Hey, it's the *kamaaina* way."

"Kamaaina?"

"Man, you really are F.O.P."

"Huh?"

"Fresh off da plane. *Kamaaina* means local." Kimo dialed, then spoke in rapid-fire pidgin into the phone. Smiling at Kate, he hung up. "It's all taken care of."

"Thanks. That's very nice of you, Kimo. I don't know what to say."

"It's nuthin. It's how tings work on dis side of da island. We one big family, ovah here."

Kate smiled and shook his hand. Then she hopped into her Jeep and headed for the Inn.

※ ※ ※

The tiny town of Waimea was just as she pictured it. It was like going back in time to old Hawaii. There was a market, two gas stations, a couple of local eateries, a movie theater—and a Subway restaurant. Oh, well. In the middle of town was a little park with picnic benches. Perfect.

Just past town was the turnoff for the Plantation Inn. You could miss it if you weren't looking for it. There was a small sign for the Westside Brewing Company, an open air bar and grill in the front of the property, and a little further down the gravel road, the entrance to the Inn. It looked open and inviting. Kate parked in the shade of a big Banyan tree.

On her way to check-in, Kate almost skipped she was so excited to be here. She tried to find the words to describe how she felt when she glanced at the grounds and out over the water. The word she came up with was "light." She felt light.

CHAPTER 3

Doc Skinner, the longtime hitting coach for the Padres, went from locker to locker in the clubhouse patting players on the back and telling a quick joke to make sure the team stayed loose as the team prepared to play the Dodgers, their rival from Los Angeles—and a hot team. Although the Dodgers trailed the first-place Padres in the standings, they were on a winning streak. The Padres had a substantial lead in the National League West race for the Pennant with more than half the season in their rearview mirror.

The team was a healthy mix of talented younger players and several savvy veterans. Everyone was excited to be a part of a pennant race, playing in one of the league's newest ballparks. Petco Park was state-of-the-art in every way—the clubhouse being no exception. It was less like a locker room and more like a living room. A giant high-definition television dominated the wall adjacent to the players' lockers. Of course it was tuned to ESPN at all times.

"We bring you breaking news from San Diego," ESPN broadcaster Todd Wright began. "Veteran Padre catcher Angel Ramirez has been charged with murdering his wife of five years. Katherine Ramirez disappeared August 10th and, despite an intensive search for her in and around San Diego, she has not been found. Authorities have not yet released the reasons why Angel Ramirez has been charged with her murder, but a source close to the investigation said they suspected foul play all along and the focus of their investigation had always been her husband."

On the screen the camera switched from photos of Kate and Angel to game footage of Angel from earlier in the season. "Ramirez was charged and booked this morning on second-degree murder in San Diego Superior Court. His arraignment hasn't been scheduled. We will be bringing you more on this story as it develops. Here to discuss the details of this latest in a string of domestic violence among professional athletes is *ESPN Baseball Tonight* analyst Taylor James, a former teammate of Ramirez."

Doc and the entire team gathered around the TV, their mouths agape. "Taylor, you played alongside Angel when you were both on the Padres and traded together to the Mets in the early '90s. Could you have predicted any of this from what you observed of Ramirez on and off the field?"

Fit, rugged, and handsome, Taylor looked like he could be playing professional baseball right now. He pondered the question. "There are always going to be players who are unable to adapt to life as a major league ballplayer and all the perks that go with it. Angel was one of the players I worried about, but this was when he first came into the league. I thought he had made some changes in his life since then. I just don't know."

"It's no secret this isn't the first time Angel has been in trouble with the law and the league, including allegations that he used steroids to prolong his playing days. Do you see this as the end of his long and controversial career?"

"I'm sure playing baseball is the least of Angel's worries right now, Todd. My wife and I knew Kate and we're both saddened by what's happened."

"This is a big concern for the Padres. They are in the middle of a pennant race. Do you think this will be a big distraction for the team?"

"This could be a huge distraction for the team if they let it. I'm guessing they'll cut Angel loose as soon as possible. This is probably the last straw as far as the team is concerned. I know they were reluctant to sign him in the first place. He is one of those players that bring a lot of baggage with him. He's been with ten different clubs in his ten plus years in the league. The team needed a veteran behind the plate and they took a gamble on Angel. It looks like it didn't pay off. The Padres now have a void to fill as they go forward from here."

"Thanks for your insights, Taylor. Let's return to our game of the week now in progress."

Doc was as stunned as anyone and for the first time in his life didn't know what to say. He looked around the locker room and for a few seconds, nobody said a word as the implications of what they'd all heard and seen sank in. Angel had a reputation as a selfish player on the field and a constant distraction off it. It drove the coaches crazy, Doc included. Fans never knew what went on behind the scenes—especially when a team was

on the road. The coaches were well aware of which players cheated on their wives and put partying ahead of
playing the following day. Angel was one of the worst
offenders anyone could recall on both counts. Yet he
was still able to get it together when the first pitch was
thrown and contributed to the Padres winning ways. In
that regard, he had the respect and admiration of the
coaches and his teammates. Now they were all left to
wonder what's next.

Veteran outfielder Brian Reynolds broke the silence. "Look, Angel hasn't been proven guilty of anything. Yeah, it looks bad, but maybe he didn't do it, the
charges will be dropped in a day or two, and he comes
back and helps us win some games."

Doc and the rest of the team nodded, but nobody
believed that. They all knew it was unlikely Angel
would get out of this one without some sort of suspen-
sion, at the very least.

"B.R. is right," said second baseman Mark Little.
He nodded toward Reynolds. "Let's just wait and see
what happens. For now, we need to focus on tonight's
game and let this thing with Angel play out."

Doc agreed. "I'm sure management is working on
getting someone in here to help out in the short term.
For now, just prepare yourself to play the Dodgers."

Several players looked toward the manager's office. As if on cue, the door opened and out walked
the team's leader, a former big league catcher himself.
"By your stunned expressions I can see you've already
heard the news. Look, it's not as bad as it seems. We've
already traded for a catcher from Seattle. The guy calls a

great game and isn't an automatic out at the plate. He's not Angel, but he'll help us keep winning games. Angel swears he didn't do it, so with any luck the charges will be dropped and he may be back behind the plate in a few games." Always a man of few words, the manager went back in his office and shut the door.

The players looked to Doc for inspiration, and he didn't disappoint them. "Look at this like Angel got hurt and can't play. If all of you pick up the pace and play a little harder, we'll continue to win, no matter who our catcher is."

Joe Sanders, a veteran of several seasons in the league, shook his head, "I don't know about you guys, but my wife is going to be all over me if half the stuff Angel did comes out in the media."

"Man, I never even thought about that," said another veteran, Ty Young. "My wife is always riding me about the shit on road. This ain't gonna help."

"Hey, Huffy," yelled outfielder Rod Johnson, "Was Kate one of the Madres?"

Those were players' wives who went out into the community and did good deeds. They also loved to attend games and gossip about the players between innings. They especially relished good gossip about some of the other wives and girlfriends, Doc knew.

"Uh, no, I don't think so. She never came to the house for meetings that I know of," said longtime Padre reliever Tim Huffman.

All the players began discussing the case and what it meant to the team and at home. Within minutes the locker room was abuzz about everything—from how

Angel did it to where he buried the body. Everyone in the clubhouse believed in Angel's guilt. Everyone.

CHAPTER 4

"Carol. CAROL!" Literary agent Sandi Golding yelled into the intercom, her voice as large as she was. The windows behind her only dulled the non-stop chatter of traffic on the midtown Manhattan street below.

"Yes, Ms. Golding," her assistant said. The uber-agent insisted on being called by her surname.

"Didn't we have a manuscript come through here about a missing baseball player or his wife or something like that?"

"Yes."

"Well, where is it?" Sandi shouted.

She has the patience of a two-year-old child with ADD, Carol thought. "You said you weren't interested, so I threw it in the slush pile," Carol said to the tyrannical agent.

Almost before Carol had finished her sentence, Sandi was now in front of her. "Well, is it still there?" Sandi demanded.

"Probably. Nobody has time to read anything around here—or mail anything back." Carol replied calmly, attempting to avert the possibility of what staffers called the "Golding shower"—when the agent would get so pissed off at you that she'd spit when she spoke.

But Sandi didn't reply and instead made her way to the enormous pile of unsolicited, and thus unread, manuscripts and book proposals in an adjacent room. "What was it called?" she yelled to Carol, as she tossed manuscripts and proposals (people's hopes and dreams) to the side.

"*Angel*." Carol answered, as she rushed in to scoop and bundle the packages Sandi was tossing around.

"That's the title? Jeez. No wonder I didn't want to pitch it. What's the author's name?"

"Katherine Ramirez."

"Ah, yes. Good. That will be all, Carol."

"Yes, Ms. Golding," Carol said.

❋ ❋ ❋

Sandi Golding rummaged through the slush pile until she found what she was looking for. She had to act quickly. Another agent may have also received a copy of the manuscript. Sandi made her way back to her desk and thumbed through her enormous Rolodex until she found the editor she was looking for.

In a voice as sweet and sincere as it had been cold and condescending minutes earlier, Sandi Golding spoke to the assistant for Thomas McGunne at Gladstone Books on the phone.

"Hi, Ginny, this is Sandi Golding. How are those beautiful dogs of yours, Fred and Ginger?"

"Wow, I can't believe you remember their names. They're both doing great, Ms. Golding. Thanks for asking. I'll put you right through to Mr. McGunne.

"Thank you, Ginny. Take care of those precious dogs."

"I will. Here you go."

"Sandi, I was just going to call you. What a month, huh?" the verbose editor said. "Our latest literary find is really taking off. I'm sure you know, her book cracked the *New York Times* bestseller list, and she hasn't even done any major media yet—it's all from the amazing reviews and the author's own grassroots campaign. Thanks again for pitching me first, Sandi. I really appreciate it."

"Tom, I always come to you first with the best and the brightest. That's why I'm calling. I have a manuscript that I know you are going to want to rush into print. It's a guaranteed runaway best seller."

"Lunch?"

"Let's meet on Friday. I have a request. Please leave your associate editor on the sidelines for this one," Sandi said, letting the somewhat putzy editor know this was not a request, but a requirement.

"Whatever you say. See you at our usual spot at noon on Friday," McGunne said.

Sandi wanted to read the manuscript, in case it was horrible and needed doctoring before she sent it via messenger the following day. She rarely read manuscripts any more, instead trusting that tiresome chore to her minions. This one, however, she would personally read. She locked her office and headed home early—it was only six o'clock. Her staffers all said goodnight but Sandi simply ignored them and headed for the elevators. She would spend the night reading the manuscript by the dead writer, killed at the hands of her famous husband—according to news reports.

CHAPTER 5

Despite the euphoria of being at the place she had been dreaming and scheming about for over a year, Kate was also a little bit scared. She looked around the parking lot of West Side Brewing Company, for what she didn't know. Checking into a hotel—even one as lax as the Plantation Inn—made her jittery.

Instead of heading straight for the lobby, she went up the wooden stairs into the brewery. It was late morning and almost nobody was there. She peered in. It looked like an old house turned into a bar and grill, except it had an odd charm about it. She couldn't put her finger on it.

Then it hit her—the place had a mid-century Hawaiian feel to it. Everything about it was how she expected Kauai to be. The place was open on all sides, surrounded by lush vegetation and a wide variety of fragrant flowers. The ceilings were vaulted with large fans circulating the warm air. The walls were lined with bamboo and the floors made from some kind of exotic wood she had never seen before.

Someone tapped her on the shoulder and she nearly jumped out of her skin. "I am so sorry," said a blonde waitress. "I was just going to see if I could seat you by the window, but I think you need to sit right here at the bar and have a drink to calm your nerves." The woman's complexion revealed the amount of time she must have spent in the Hawaiian sun in her younger years. When she smiled, her tan and weathered face creased at all the right (and wrong) places.

Kate gave a crooked smile and said, "You know what, that's a really good idea."

"The first drink is on me. What'll it be?" The waitress had a warm and friendly glow about her, helped by her bright floral sundress.

Kate almost said white wine but realized that was what she would have ordered in her past life. What would her new and improved self order? "I'll have a beer," she blurted, shocked by her answer.

A beer? Well, it was a start.

"How about a pale ale?" the waitress asked.

"Perfect." Not really sure what a pale ale was, but willing to give it a try.

"We serve food at the bar, too. Here's a menu. My name is Lulu. You know, like Honolulu? My mom was a travel agent and loved Hawaii."

"Thanks, Lulu," Kate said. She didn't offer to give her name. How suspicious might that seem?

Kate sipped her pale ale and enjoyed a cheeseburger and fries. This was so not her, but she was done with dieting, personal trainers, and spin classes just to please Angel, who still called her fat, even though she was more fit than he was. No, the new Kate would be down to earth, real, and if she kept up this diet, probably a little chunky, too.

"You feeling a little less jumpy?" Lulu brought the check.

"Yeah, thanks. I feel a lot better." Kate paid in cash and left a generous tip, then headed to the lobby. She had a nice beer buzz and it wasn't even happy hour yet. She was feeling a lot better. Checking into the Inn was a pivotal point in establishing her new life and she didn't want to blow it with a case of the nerves.

※ ※ ※

Although the brewery stood alone, the lobby was literally right next door, through a short breezeway. When she got halfway to the lobby, Kate stared to her left, awestruck by the scene. There were dozens of palm trees spread out over a grassy area at least three football fields long. Along the edges of the grass were individual cottages that looked like quaint little houses painted to perfection. Every cottage had a deck and large comfortable wicker chairs facing the large lawn and beyond that, the beach. A perfectly positioned pool stretched out at the far end of the property. Hammocks strung between several of the palm trees overlooked the ocean. On the other side of the lobby, a red cottage converted to a day spa was surrounded by foliage for privacy; a simple sign read, *Massages*. That was a luxury she might allow herself once she settled in.

On her way to the lobby, Kate passed through an open-air reading room that seemed the perfect place to spend an afternoon curled up on one of the comfy chairs. Her heart soared. She had the unmistakable sensation that this was like the best day of summer back on the mainland, only it was going to last all year. Kate took a deep breath and walked into the lobby, a trip back in time.

She gazed at the framed history of this important property on the walls, then perused the museum and gift shop. On the walls were early photos of plantation workers and their families. Kate studied the old photographs, entranced.

When she did finally inch her way toward the reception area, a beautiful young Hawaiian woman with a flower behind her ear looked up from her computer and smiled warmly. Kate was easily this nervous when she boarded the flight to the islands using her new (and very costly) identification, but she got through it. So she walked up to the counter and confidently said, "I'm checking in."

"I know. I'm Vina," the Inn employee said. When Kate stared blankly at her, she added, "You met my uncle Kimo at Salt Pond."

"He really called you?" Kate rapped her forehead. "Wow!"

"Of course." Vina leaned over the counter and whispered, "I saved you the nicest cottage we have. It's way in the back so if you have a puppy, he won't bother anyone."

"Thank you, Vina. I don't know if I'm going to go back for the puppy. He was very cute, though. Maybe I will. We'll see."

"Either way, you'll like this unit. It's quiet and secluded. Here, let me show you where it is." Vina got out a map of the property printed on parchment to make it look old. Circling the lobby on the map, she said, "You are here, and the 'Hemingway House' is here." Vina circled one of the larger squares, standing alone in the far corner of the property. "The cottages are all set apart for privacy, but this particular unit is special, a converted house off by itself. It's a favorite of several other writers—that's how it got its name."

"I can see why. It really is secluded." Kate stared at the circled spot on the map that would be her new home. She had researched the property online and knew this was a very popular accommodation at the Inn. She couldn't believe it was available. It had everything—a large living room, kitchen and even a dining room, all with an ocean view. She doubted Earnest Hemingway ever stayed there, but knew other well-known authors had signed the underside of the writing table in the spare room. Kate couldn't wait to see whose name might be scribbled there.

"You can park right here," Vina said, indicating a private spot right next to the cottage. "The pool is here, there is a big open room right here if you enjoy morning yoga, and the Brewery next door is open late if you want to hang out at night. Of course, the ocean is here," Vina said as she pointed to the shoreline that butted up against the property. Her room was only steps from the black sand beach.

It was Kate's turn to lean in. "How did you know I'm a writer?"

"I didn't, but we get so many, it's always a good guess." Vina smiled. "Not many tourists want a place with no radio, no phone, no TV, and no Internet access any more."

"Not a problem," Kate said.

"Good. We do have all of those things in the recreation room if you feel the need. And when it rains, which unfortunately isn't that often on this side of the island, the sound of the drops hitting the tin roof of the rec room creates a peaceful sound. You can watch the sunset over Ni'hau while you check your e-mail from there."

"No, no. I'm looking forward to the peace and quiet. I'm here to get away from the distractions of modern life so I can focus on my writing."

"Good for you. Okay, all I need you to do is fill in this registration card." Vina passed her the form.

Kate started writing in her name, her real name. She quickly crumpled up the card and asked for another.

"It doesn't really matter what you put down. Most writers use fake names when they check in."

Kate smiled and asked, "Can I pay cash for the room, Vina?"

"Of course," Vina winked.

"Good. That's good." Kate pulled a stack of hundreds from her purse.

CHAPTER 6

"I read the manuscript. Not bad. Not bad at all," said Thomas McGunne, a well-seasoned editor who was adept at spotting and acquiring new talent. Yet, just like a poker player with a good hand, he had to play it cool. From the glint in his eyes he thought the book was one of the best he's read in a really long time. Good, Sandi thought, she had him by the balls.

"The author shows a lot of potential. The plot is strong, the pacing brisk, and she pulls the reader along nicely. I like the dialogue—it's crisp, believable, and original. The protagonist is likeable, and you find yourself hoping she escapes the grasp of her horrible husband. And the ending, well, it's brilliant. I think it's possible you've found a writer readers will connect with... but you never know." A good actor, the editor shrugged.

Sandi smiled, knowing she had him. "I know. It's a runaway best seller, for sure."

"Maybe. Is the author the woman who was killed by her husband, the ballplayer?"

"Yup," said Sandi.

"Interesting," McGunne said, pulling on his beard.

"There's your media hook right there. This book will make a killing with an angle like that, don't you agree?"

"A killing?" he asked with raised eyebrows.

"Okay, bad choice of words. But it doesn't take a genius to see the potential for a book by a murdered woman with a famous husband—who you've already acknowledged can really write. Now that she's dead, the media is making her more famous than her husband."

McGunne knew he was being sold, but he had to admit the publicity would push the book right up the bestseller list. "We would still need someone to go around and talk the book up on the usual shows. Does the author have any relatives we could tap for the talk shows?"

"Not that I know of. No kids, her parents are both deceased, and her husband is in jail for her murder," Sandi said, not quite sure if what she got from a quick Google search was accurate, but what the hell.

"You have the exclusive rights to negotiate this deal then?" McGunne asked.

"Of course. My author agreement has a disclaimer in the event the author dies. Since there are no surviving heirs that I know of, the rights revert back to the agency," Sandi said with a grin. This was a lie, and one she would have to correct with a fabricated contract, but it's nothing she hadn't done before.

"Lucky you. So what kind of advance are you looking for?"

"$500,000."

"Out of the question."

"What were you going to offer?"

"I can go to $250,000 without having to get approval," the editor said as he pushed his spectacles in place and smoothed his sweater vest.

Sandi smiled. She had anticipated the terms and the dollar amount to the penny and had her counterproposal ready. "I'll take $450,000, but I want it all up front. I also want ten percent of the cover price, not the usual seven point five. This manuscript needs very little work and we need to get it out now. There's no author to slow things down and I am a lot more amiable than any writer would be. The sooner this hits bookstores, the better."

"Jesus, Sandi. You don't have to do a damn thing and you don't even have to pay the author her 85 percent of the advance," McGunne griped. "I love books and the book business." After years of reading manuscripts into the wee hours of the morning and on weekends—this after working 14-hour days—he was fortunate to have achieved his rather lofty position in trade publishing, but he also knew he would never see this kind of money himself. His pay felt paltry compared to some of the major deals he'd inked, and especially for the cost of living In Manhattan, but he always felt privileged to work in this business—until this moment. For some reason this deal bothered him.

Sandi quickly sensed his trepidation and reminded him how this would play in New York's publishing circles. She also pointed out that he was getting a good deal and could brag that he landed the book of the year for under $500,000. McGunne got that old familiar feeling back by realizing once again he would be the talk of the town—at least within publishing industry—for finding the Holy Grail, a first-time author who receives rave reviews and strong sales her first time out. That kind of cachet was like money in the bank.

"It's still a lot of money for a first-time author, Sandi," he felt obligated to say.

"That's true, but look at how quickly this negotiation is going without the author involved."

"Sure, but let's see how well the book sells without the author around to promote it."

"Thomas, I can easily take this to another editor who wants a slam dunk to boost their profit-and-loss statement for years to come."

"There's no need for that. You have a deal. Get me the electronic version of the manuscript as soon as you can," Thomas said, relieved to have landed the book and anxious to get going on the project.

"Done."

"We still need a face to put forward. Someone to promote the book who either knew the author or is in some way tied in."

"I'll do it," Sandi said.

"You?"

"Yeah, I knew her as well as anyone. I mean, I was her agent for Christ's sake." This was stretching the truth, to be sure. Sandi had met Kate at a writer's conference for a few minutes and asked her to send her manuscript. That was the extent of it. She had charged Kate a reading fee to look at her manuscript and another fee for representation, and had her sign a letter of agreement. In Sandi's mind, this kind of arrangement wasn't a scam. She had overhead and a staff to pay. These fees covered her costs. The fact that she hadn't got around to reading many (if any) manuscripts was due to her hustling to make and maintain contacts in the publishing world and servicing her big-name clients. She had been too busy to reply to any of Kate's letters or calls over the past year. Sandi continued: "I discovered her and now I will help her reach her goal of being a bestselling author and novelist. That was her dream. I will tell her tragic story."

"Speaking of her tragic story," the editor started, "her protagonist escapes to a tropical island. Have you considered that the author could still be alive and sipping piña coladas in a warmer climate somewhere?"

"Just messenger the contract over to my office by the end of the day and we have a deal," Sandi said, dismissing the idea her new cash cow was sunning herself somewhere. "She's dead and her famous husband did it. This is the just the kind of scandalous thing that sells books."

In reality, Sandi wasn't as confident as she appeared. The author very well could be alive and kicking somewhere in the tropics and nothing would bring her back to the fold faster than seeing her book sitting atop the *New York Times* bestseller list. Between her lunch meeting and arrival back to the office, Sandi had formulated a plan to ensure she got the glory and the greenbacks. Walking past her assistant's desk—who was busy eating a sandwich she had brought from home and answering the phone between bites—Sandi said without a *hello* or *how are you*, "That mob guy whose memoir we were working on. You know, the guy who won't stop bugging me about his book. Get him on the phone."

Before Carol could respond, Sandi was in her office

and shut the door. "Bitch," Carol said quietly, pieces of her sandwich falling into her lap. But what Carol didn't know was how impressed Sandi was with her work. Sandi didn't dare tell her. The minute her assistant realized she had a future in this business, she would leave—and Sandi needed her. So any chance Sandi got, she kept her assistant down to keep her around.

A few minutes later, Carol buzzed Sandy. "Tony Gravano is on line one." No *thank you*, nothing. Just click.

But when Sandi picked up the line to talk to Tony she was sweet as could be. "How are you?" She patiently listened as her crook-turned-wannabe author went on and on about his frustrations with the publishing process. He was sharing stories of others in his writing group who were getting publishing deals and wanted to know how long it would be before he could get an advance for his own crime novel—which was based on real crimes, namely his own.

"Well, I have some great news. I have some interest from Harper Collins in your book."

"Oh my God, that is so great. How much did they offer?" Tony asked immediately. Lord knows he needed the money.

"Well, that's just it. You are a first-time author and they want you to make some changes to your manuscript. Nothing big, but before we go to contract they'd like to see a revised version."

"What kind of changes are we talkin' about?" Tony asked rather apprehensively.

"Just some plot and pacing things. I could do it for you if you'd like," Sandi said earnestly, even though it was a complete lie.

"Really? That would be great. Sandi, you're the best. I owe you big time."

"No problem. There is something you could do for me."

"You name it."

"Can you meet me at Peabody's in an hour?"

"I'll be there," Tony said, clearly on cloud nine now that he was going to be published. He went to the bathroom and, looking in the mirror, began rehearsing what he would say when his book came out and he made his first of many appearances on TV.

CHAPTER 7

"Look Angel, it's not like you were denied bail," his attorney pointed out as they talked in a room inside the courthouse.

"Five million dollars cash or bond, what kind of crap is that? I don't have that kind of money."

"You don't need the full $5 million. You just need to come up with ten percent in cash or put up collateral equal to the balance," the attorney patiently explained.

"I still can't do it," Angel said.

Now the attorney was wondering how he was going to get paid.

"How much can you get your hands on, Angel?" The attorney asked—his pen poised to write the magic number on his yellow legal pad.

"Doesn't it matter to anyone that I didn't do it?" Angel pleaded while pacing around the room.

"Actually, no. You pleaded 'not guilty' but . . ."

"How about the team? Did you talk to the owner about putting up the money for my bail?"

"I did talk to their general counsel and quite frankly the team is trying to distance themselves from this whole mess."

"Figures. Fuckers. Do you know that not one of my

teammates has come to see me?" Angel stated, not really surprised, but angry anyway.

"I think the team has moved on. Even if you were to get out on bail today I doubt they would take you back. They just traded for Red Sox catcher Don Wilson. Their plan is for him to take over for you for the remainder of the season."

"Don Wilson! He can't hit for shit. They signed Don fucking Wilson. Unbelievable. Don't think I won't remember who was on my side and who stabbed me in the back when I needed them the most when this whole goddamn thing is over and I'm a free man."

Angel's attorney said nothing.

"What a friggin' nightmare. I'm innocent! You believe me, don't you?"

"Sure, Angel, but I need to get a better handle on your finances to see how to proceed. We need to put a team together for your defense and that costs money. So, I have to ask, how much money can you come up with for your defense?"

"My money is none of your business."

"As your attorney, it is. I'm sure you've heard of attorney/client confidentiality. I can't and won't discuss or disclose your financial matters with anyone you don't want me to. So, I need to know what we're dealing with here. Let's start with cash. How much cash do you have access to?"

"Cash? You can't use this against me, right? Well, I've been stashing some cash to keep it away from the old lady. Good thing I did, too. I've got about $25,000. That's it. That *puta* bled me dry. She spent every dime

I made. I could fucking kill . . ." Angel caught himself and mumbled, "kill myself for not putting Kate on an allowance like the other players' wives."

Angel's attorney clearly looked uncomfortable and tried to recover. He resented having to represent the Angel Ramirezes of the world. However, he took his work seriously, which meant dealing with the good and bad of pro sports. So, until such time as Angel was unable to pay his fee or fires him—and he hoped that was going to happen soon—he would stick it out. He looked at Angel as he paced around the room in his bright orange jumpsuit, playing with his goatee.

"Hey, what about life insurance?" Angel asked. "When we got married I remember taking out a policy on her for something like $750,000."

The attorney was thinking to himself, great, there's all the motive the District Attorney needs to convince a jury that an aging, broke ballplayer killed his wife for the money. "Angel, I don't think you're going to be able to collect on that policy considering the current circumstances. Besides, the county coroner won't issue a death certificate without a body for six months." The attorney opened a file and pulled out some documents. "What about the house you bought two years ago? There's got to be some equity there."

"Nah, I took out a second and a third mortgage on it."

"Okay, how about your cars?"

"Leased," Angel said quickly, clearly deep in thought.

The attorney flipped through the pages. "How

about your boat."

"I took out the second on the house to buy the boat."

"Angel, about my fee . . ." the attorney started to ask but was cut off.

"Wait! WAIT! You said the coroner won't issue a death certificate for six months without a body. Right?"

"Right. They want to be certain the party in question is actually dead."

"Exactly. Exactly! That's it! Kate's not dead. She's… she's alive!" Angel slammed his hand on the table as a deputy opened the door and looked in. The attorney waved him away.

"Oh my God. That's it. She's not dead," Angel said shaking his head.

"What are you saying? Of course she's dead. The evidence…"

"Fuck the evidence. I told you, I didn't kill her."

His attorney just sat there staring at Angel as he bounced around the room like a kid on Christmas morning.

"She's alive. That bitch is alive somewhere, I know it. I can feel it. I've got to find her. If I find her, then I'm off the hook. That's it. That's how I get out of this mess," Angel said, his mind racing with possibilities now. He continued to pace the room talking it through, full of hope and enthusiasm. "I can't believe it. Why didn't I think of it sooner? Why didn't you think of it?" Angel said glaring and pointing at his attorney.

The thought of representing an innocent man suddenly got the attorney's juices flowing, too. "I don't know how I missed it, but you're right. If Kate is alive and we can find her..." his voiced trailed off as he was also lost in thought.

"You're fired," Angel said.

"What?"

"You're fired. You haven't done shit. Take a hike."

"What about the appeal on your bail?" Now that he was somewhat convinced Angel may not be a murderer, the thought of a high-profile trial had some appeal to him. He saw himself on *Larry King Live* and some of the other major interview shows, as well as the national news.

"Forget it," Angel said, glaring at him in a very intimidating way. "I'll get a public defender to handle my appeal."

Undeterred, the attorney said, "This is just the kind of thing the court will have to take into consideration."

"What are you still doing here? I thought I just fired you."

The attorney was stunned.

"Guard. Guard!" Angel screamed. He wanted to get to a phone. He knew just the guy to find Kate and bring her back—and it would be a lot cheaper than his lame-ass attorney would be.

CHAPTER 8

Almost every day, Kate hopped in her Jeep to explore the island of Kauai. She went to every single beach from Barking Sands and Polihale on the far west side of the island to Moloa'a and Tunnels, the best beaches on the north shore, and everywhere in between. Whenever she could, she would either snorkel, swim, or bodysurf in the warm, clear water and take a midday nap in the cool sand under one of the many palm trees lining the shore. She also enjoyed hiking and walked most of the more accessible trails around the island. The Inn was only a few miles from Koke'e State Park and some of Kauai's best trails, featuring stunning waterfalls and jaw-dropping views such as Waimea Canyon, commonly known as the "Grand Canyon of the Pacific." Vina's uncle Kimo taught Kate how to surf at two different breaks on the west side—Majors and Picalas. But Kate preferred to rent a board from the Marriott on Kalapaki Bay and paddle out to the beginner break located right out in front. After catching a few waves she could relax on the grassy area next to Duke's. In Kapaa she kayaked on the Wailua river and stumbled onto Kauai's semi-secret nude beach. Kate's favorite thing to do during the day was lounge under one of the many big banyan trees found around the island, have a picnic lunch and read one of the books she borrowed from the Inn's library. She preferred places in town for lunch, but would sometimes wander into Old Koloa or Lihue for a bite. These were a little more local, and the chance of bumping into someone who knew her from her other life was less likely.

The nights were long, lonely ones. She loved the tranquility and isolation of her remote hideaway, but missed some of the energy of the evening on the mainland. She was restless, but had no regrets of making the move to Kauai. After watching the sunset from the deck of her cottage each night, Kate found new and creative ways to put off writing her next novel. These included cleaning her cottage (even though housekeeping was provided), washing her Jeep (even though the rich, red dirt would be back on it within minutes), or talking story with the staff (most of whom were enablers when it came to procrastination). Without realizing it, she had fallen into the routine of watching the sunset and then heading over to the bar for a beer. She became such a regular that the waitresses, bartenders, and cooks (who knew her by her assumed name, Kay) made it a point to pass her and say hello or stop and chat. Tonight was no exception, except that Lulu came over and said something that would change Kate's life.

"Hey, Kay, what are you doing tonight?" Lulu asked while balancing a tray full of dirty dishes.

Kate gave her a look that said, *Puleeze. You know the answer to that.*

"I see. Not much going on, eh? Could you fill in for Rita? She can't come in tonight."

"Me?" Kate said, almost looking behind her to check and see if Lulu meant to ask someone else.

"Yeah, you. You're here enough to know your way around," Lulu said, shifting the tray to the other shoulder.

Trying to stall, Kate asked, "So, what happened to Rita?"

"Who knows with that one? More drama than I can handle. It's something with her boyfriend. I didn't really listen when she called. We were already short-handed tonight. Look at me, I'm bussing tables," Lulu said, nodding to the tray teetering on her shoulder—which wasn't getting any lighter. "So, what do you think?"

"Lulu, I don't know. I've never worked in a restaurant before." That was the truth. Kate never really had a regular job to speak of. She never needed to. Her parents, previous boyfriends, and finally Angel always paid for everything. Kate's stomach was doing flips. What if someone vacationing from San Diego came in for dinner and recognized her? This would be a big risk. On the other hand, they could just as easily bump into her in the bathroom of the Brewery. The whole experience of leaving Angel and starting a new life was to become more independent. What better way to do that than working for a living? Besides, she was bored and the thought of doing something productive that forced her outside of her comfort zone was intriguing.

Kate was deep in thought as Lulu put her arm around her and said, "You can do it. Come on, I'll show you what to do before it gets too busy." Lulu put the her tray down and steered Kate toward the hostess stand at the top of the stairs, making it easy to greet guests as they entered the restaurant. To Kate it felt like she was out on an island—staring down a steep cliff. She was terrified. After a few minutes of on-the-job training, Lulu was off serving customers and Kate was left to fend for herself. Fortunately, all the waitresses were willing to help show her the ropes. Kate did her best to warmly greet customers, trying not to let on she had no idea what she was doing, and seat them where it made the most sense to her. Before she knew it, the dinner rush was over.

All the waitresses gathered around the bar to total out the night's receipts and have a drink or three. Kate sat down on a barstool with a smile from ear to ear. She listened to the banter back and forth between the employees of the Westside Brewing Company and sipped a beer. Each waitress took turns complimenting Kate on a job well done. Kate soaked it all in. So, this is what work is like. Even though she was tired, it was a good kind of tired. She felt better than she had in a long time. When the girls all asked if she could work on Saturday night, too, Kate shrugged *why not?* One of the bartenders brought her a shot of tequila to do with the rest of the employees. Kate finally felt like she belonged, looking around at the group as they joked and laughed like they didn't have a care in the world. The girls here all had a lot less money and worldly possessions than all of her "friends" back home—most of the girls here didn't even own cars. They walked or rode their bikes wherever they needed to go. When anyone of them did have a car, it was always a contest to see whose had the most rust and cost the least. They learned to live with less, and in many ways they were better for it. When she really thought about it, she had been one of those whiny, neurotic, and chronically unhappy women when she was hanging out with some of the other players' wives. Those women had all the trappings of success and certainly looked the part, but for the most part they were miserable. The fact that she was no longer a part of that world and now a part of this one gave Kate a warm, fuzzy feeling. She looked around and took a mental snapshot to be able to remember this moment in case she was ever tempted to go back to her old life. It was a warm tropical night with the light breeze causing the flames from the tiki torches to dance against the dark sky. Every night on Kauai was special, but this one was decidedly different. It would take a lot to get her to leave this.

"Kay, are you gonna do your shot or just sit there grinning like you just won the lottery?" Lulu asked.

"Oh, duh," Kate said as she raised her glass and gulped down the smoothest shot she had ever done.

"Good, eh? No need for training wheels," the bartender said as he removed the salt and lime.

Lulu whispered in Kate's ear, "Speaking of winning the lottery, here's your tips and wages. I hope you don't mind, but we like to pay our hostesses under the table."

Kate hadn't even thought about getting paid and turned to Lulu and insisted, "Oh no, no, no. You don't owe me anything."

"We owe you a lot. You came through for us tonight. You're a natural. You have a future here," Lulu said and they both laughed.

Kate felt the wad of cash in her palm. It felt good. It also felt like a lot of money. In reality, it was just over $100, but with the way she was blowing through her cash, a little extra money would come in handy. Kate decided at that moment that she would accept any hours the brewery offered her. Working wasn't bad. In fact, it was the best she'd felt about herself in a long time and she savored the moment because, based on her history, she knew it wouldn't last long… and it didn't.

CHAPTER 9

"The body has yet to be found, but our sources tell us it's just a matter of time before the remains of Katherine Ramirez are discovered," the overly dramatic CNM host stated to her viewers. "We turn to forensic expert Dr. John Stevens for this report.

"Thanks, Stacy. It seems the San Diego Police have a wealth of forensic evidence that not only proves Katherine Ramirez is dead, but points to her husband Angel Ramirez as the prime suspect."

"That's quite a statement, Dr. Stevens. Elaborate for us," the host said, clearly leading her "witness," even though the lawyer-turned-media-star hadn't been in a courtroom in over a decade.

"It seems portions of her scalp and other body parts were recovered at the crime scene," John Stevens stated, confident that the information was accurate, since he had paid good money to obtain it.

"The crime scene being the domicile of the happy couple," the host and former prosecutor injected with far more drama and conviction than was called for.

On cue the forensic expert replied with authority, "Yes, they found blood splatters everywhere, a bloody shirt belonging to the defendant, and that portion of her scalp. DNA tests confirmed it belonged to Mrs. Ramirez."

"It doesn't look good for Mr. Ramirez, does it, John?"

"No, it doesn't. I'd say this is a textbook case of domestic abuse that got out of hand and escalated to murder."

"I agree. Thank you, Dr. Stevens."

"We now go to Juan Rivera. Juan, I understand you were able to talk to Angel Ramirez."

"That's right. My impression of him is that he is overly hostile and hiding something," Rivera reported as he stood outside the jailhouse for effect.

"I think you are on to something, Juan. Mr. Ramirez has a criminal record as long as his throwing arm. CNM has uncovered documents that show he is a predicate felon and has on previous occasions assaulted women. It's not a stretch to assume he could murder his wife."

"I agree, Stacy. While I was inside, I talked to a couple of his fellow inmates who confirmed he all but admitted beating his wife."

"Wow! You heard it here on CNM: Angel Ramirez admits he beat his wife. Thank you for that report, Juan."

"This is Juan Rivera reporting from outside the San Diego jail."

"If I were prosecuting this case, I guarantee you I would be able to convict with the evidence we have been presented with on this show. Join us tomorrow when we talk to San Diego Padres manager Bob Skinner, as well as the team's equipment manager. You won't want to miss this. This is Stacy Gray, and we'll see you back here tomorrow with more startling details regarding the disappearance and apparent murder of Kate Ramirez at the hands of her husband, baseball star Angel Ramirez."

CHAPTER 10

Kate soaked in the tropical night air and became part of the banter between the bartenders and waitresses. She knew them well enough now to poke fun in a friendly way. Sipping her beer, she was starting to feel the effects of the tequila shot take hold.

"Can I get a beer?" came a voice from behind as someone slid in next to her.

"Here you go, Bob," Dan the bartender said as he slid a Barking Beer down the bar. Dan also made eye contact with Kate and with a quick nod in the direction of the guy with the beer indicated as subtly as possible she should watch herself. Dan grabbed some dirty beer glasses and began the methodical process of washing, drying, and hanging them in the overhead rack, but made sure Kate got the message with a raised eyebrow.

Kate frowned and mouthed back a "what?"

"Thanks, Dan," Bob said as he turned to Kate and asked, "Don't I know you from somewhere?"

Kate's heart stopped. She didn't dare look at the man to her left. Thankfully, Dan jumped in to help.

"Bob, is that some kind of pick-up line? Because if it is, I don't want you harassing the help, if you get my meaning."

Undeterred, Bob pressed on. "Seriously, you look so familiar to me," he said while trying to get a better look at Kate's face. "Are you from San Diego?"

Again, Kate froze. She was in panic mode staring straight down at the Koa wood of the bar, unable to speak or move.

"Hey, Bob, the lady isn't interested. All right?" Dan asked, as he put is palms of his hands on top of the bar and leaned in. Years of being a bartender taught him how to deal with people like Bob. The fact that Bob was a popular musician from the mainland didn't mean a thing to Dan, who had been a minor celebrity as a one-time professional beach volleyball player (during the years when you could make a living from the sport and routinely see yourself on national TV). He kept in shape by playing pick-up games on the volleyball courts on the grounds of the Inn. Dan maintained a muscular six-foot-five-inch frame that was as tough as nails. Bob, on the other hand, was a soft five-foot-five inches "tall" with long greasy hair and a perpetual five o'clock shadow. It was clear who would win if a fight broke out between the two of them. Dan could count on one hand the times he actually had to take action against an unruly customer. His size and steely demeanor usually was a deterrent for even the drunkest customer. Bob didn't seem drunk, but was more of a persistent pain in the ass.

Bob stared at Dan thinking about saying something smart but instead meekly said, "Look, I play at this place in San Diego called the Baja Cantina. It's a restaurant and bar overlooking the Island Marina where I lived aboard my sailboat and, I swear, she looks just like someone I've seen at the bar and on her boat. I'm sorry, I must be mistaken." Bob pounded his beer and took out his tip money to pay for his overpriced drink. He then wheeled his guitar and amp to the parking lot without further incident.

Kate was so shaken she could barely get up from the barstool.

"You okay? Need a glass of water?" Dan asked. Kate looked like she could faint at any moment.

Kate tried to compose herself before she spoke. "Thanks for sticking up for me," was all she could say. She was afraid that if she said any more she would puke right there.

"It's nothing. On this side of the island we don't like people poking around about our pasts," Dan said. "There's plenty of us here trying to escape someone or something, so we have a don't-ask-don't-tell policy when it comes to where we're from or what we did before we got here. Me? Let's just say there are more then a few jealous husbands who would like to play volleyball with my head."

Kate chuckled and said, "Uh, I don't know what to say, Dan. Thank you. I'm going back to my bungalow. I'll see you tomorrow."

"Do you want that water to go?" Dan asked, already filling a plastic cup with ice.

"That'd be nice," Kate said, avoiding eye contact as she accepted the water. She was so freaked out by what happened she couldn't be sure who she could trust.

Lulu came over. "You leaving?" she asked.

"Yeah. After tonight, I have a lot of respect for you

and the girls, Lulu. Working in the restaurant biz is a lot harder than it looks. I hope I didn't let you down."

"Come here, Kay," Lulu said with her arms out-stretched. "Let me tell you something," she slurred. "You were sooooo good. Give me a hug, okay." Lulu didn't wait for an answer and gave Kate a big bear hug. "You really came through for us, girl. Now go get some sleep and I'll see you tomorrow."

Kate was on autopilot and mumbled something and waved goodbye. She started walking gingerly to-ward the door, her legs like rubber. The same warm tropical night that offered so much promise only min-utes ago now felt heavy, as if laced with fear and dread. Her mind raced with her options as she slowly walked across the grass to her cottage. She didn't want to leave her life here, but she might have no choice. If she waited too long to leave, one call from Bob could bring Angel and her past right to this spot. Or Bob could be con-vinced that he was wrong. Kate's hair was short and blonde, not brown and long. She had gained at least ten pounds since San Diego. Must be the burgers and beers. Why didn't she say something to Bob back at the bar to get rid of him when she had the chance? She could have put an end to this before it even began by simply saying, "Nope, I'm actually from New Jersey, you jerk, so get the hell out of my face."

It was a pitch-black night and she had not been out this late before. It was a long walk from the restaurant to her room across the large lawn. Now thoroughly para-noid, every sound seemed suspicious.

"Relax," she told herself, "Just get to a safe place

and think things through. It'll be fine."

Suddenly, Bob stepped out from behind a hibiscus plant and startled her. Kate let out a piercing scream, but the trade winds kept it from reaching the other rooms.

Bob put his hands up and said, "Hey, it's me, Bob, from the bar. You know, the guitar guy. I just want to talk you."

"What were you doing hiding in the bushes?" Kate asked as she pushed Bob with both hands, nearly knocking him over.

"I wasn't hiding. I was waiting for you," Bob said calmly, which made Kate's skin crawl.

Kate realized she was now clutching her shirt in the front and pulling it up to her chin and she released her grip—slightly. She started walking in the direction of her room and then realized that was a mistake and turned around and headed back to the bar with Bob trailing after her, keeping his distance but not letting her get away either.

"Can you stop for a second so we can talk?" he asked.

Now that Kate was close enough to hear voices coming from inside the restaurant, she felt safer. She wheeled around and asked, "What do you want with me?"

Bob abruptly stopped. "Don't you remember me?" he said. "My boat was right across from yours at the Island Marina. A Hunter sailboat with green canvas, white dinghy, and *Sommer Time* painted on the transom. You were on C-Dock. A big Sea Ray Sundancer, the *Angel Baby*, I believe. Wasn't your husband's name Angel, and didn't he play for the Padres?"

Fortunately for Kate, Bob and his former band had been on tour while the media focused on her disappearance and probable death. He had no clue why she was pretending not to be who she was. In fact, he was starting to wonder if he was wrong, maybe this lady just looked a lot like Kate Ramirez from San Diego.

"I don't know what you're talking about," Kate said as convincingly as she could.

Bob studied her face closely in the dim glow of the lights that guided patrons to the bathrooms, which were separate from the restaurant. He decided to play along.

"Wow, then you have a sister in San Diego who could be your twin except that she has long dark hair and is a lot thinner," Bob said, not realizing how that could be construed. "I apologize. I'm really sorry. Really. Can we start over? My name is Bob Sommers, maybe you've heard of me?" He stuck out his hand and Kate hesitantly reached out and shook it.

Clearly this was one unbalanced individual, and Kate knew she needed to proceed with extreme caution. She decided to go along with his newfound niceness, despite the comment about her weight. "It's pleasure to meet you, Bob. You just scared me back there coming out of the bushes like that."

"I'm really sorry I frightened you. No hard feelings, okay?"

"It's okay. Look, I'm really tired and I think I'm just gonna go say goodbye to Dan and Lulu and then head home."

"Yeah, of course. I, uh, didn't catch your name," Bob said.

"Kay," Kate said, not offering up a last name.

"Oh, well, the woman you reminded me of is named Kate," Bob said with a wave of his hand. "Close, but obviously not the same name."

"Okay. Well, it's been nice chatting with you, Bob," Kate said as casually as she could. That was way too easy, she thought. He must be on to her. Her legs were shaking and she just wanted to get away from this creep as fast as she could. Turning and walking away, Bob called out to her.

"I'll see you Saturday, then."

Kate stopped walking and turned to face him, furrowing her brow, not sure what to do or say next.

"I saw your name on the roster for Saturday night," Bob said. "You're hostessing, and I'm playing two sets from eight to eleven."

"Oh, right, I forgot." Trying to sound cheery, she added, "See you Saturday." Then, fighting the urge to run, she walked briskly to the safety of the building instead of her bungalow.

From the dark, she heard Bob call out, "Goodnight, Kate."

CHAPTER 11

Mary Valentine was a longtime Deputy District Attorney in San Diego. She had handled many homicides, but this was her first "no body" case. While not unheard of, they were quite rare—only about 350 in the entire history of the United States. And as far as she could determine, this was the first ever in San Diego County. That it also happened to involve a local pro athlete made the case that much more intense.

Nonetheless, she felt good about the circumstantial evidence; it was on par with that of the successful "no body" murder convictions she had researched. And her District Attorney Investigators were coming up with additional bits and pieces each day—one of which led her to want to take another look at the boat Angel and Kate owned and kept in slip C-17 at the Island Marina.

Mary was well acquainted with the marina, which straddled the water next to the tall Hyatt along Mission Bay. Her friend Christie Hollingsworth had lived on a sailboat there for years, and she and her husband still had a boat there. In fact, slip C-17 was only a couple of boats down from theirs. Mary bounced the keys in her hand, excited to get out of the office and go to the marina and still call it work. It was a gorgeous day, even by

San Diego standards. She threw the evidence bag containing the keys in her purse and headed off. She debated whether or not to call Christie to tell her she'd be at the marina but decided against it.

❄ ❄ ❄

Walking down C-dock, Mary admired the boats as she always did, wondering what people had to do to afford some of the nicer ones. She certainly wasn't making that kind of money working in the D.A.'s office. To launch a possible second career, she had started and stopped writing a novel, a legal thriller. Maybe that was her ticket to a better life. She could always go to the "dark side" (private practice), but she knew that wouldn't do it for her. Mary loved the law and preferred sitting at the prosecutor's table, regardless of the long hours and pay that would probably never match what she could earn in a law firm. She was the one who made sure criminals were punished for their crimes and locked up so they can't harm anyone while serving out their sentences. Was there a more noble profession? Probably. With all the plea bargains and deals, she often wondered what she was doing and which side was the right side. She was a hard ass—no doubt about it. Around the courthouse her nickname was Maximum Mary, because she almost always sought the maximum sentence when trying a case and was difficult to deal with if you were a defense attorney seeking some sort of deal for your client. This would also explain why at age 36 she was still hopelessly single. So lost in thought, Mary walked right by *Angel Baby* and almost walked off the end of the dock.

A man with an official-looking shirt and cap stopped her and said, "Can I help you?"

"Oh, I'm okay," Mary said, looking around to get her bearings back.

"Mary?" Mary looked back at him, puzzled. "I'm Les David, the dock master. We met at the Memorial Day dock party. You're a friend of Taylor and Christie's."

"Oh, right. Les. Of course. I'm sorry, I was kinda daydreaming," Mary said as she waved her hands in the air.

"Are you here to see Christie?" the dock master inquired.

"Uh, no. I'm actually here in my capacity as a prosecutor. I need to take another look at Angel Ramirez's boat."

Les nodded, pulled at his cap, and said, "I hope I'm not out of line saying this, but I was never a fan of Angel's—on the field and otherwise. Kate, she was a doll, one of the sweetest, nicest people who passed through here. She deserved better than that."

"Did you know her well?" Mary asked, pulling out a small notepad and pen from her purse. Though the police had already talked to Les, she wanted to be prepared for any little clue that might come out.

"As a matter of fact, I did. Kate came down to the docks a lot. She was practically a live-aboard—especially during the off-season, to get away from her husband while he was at home. She'd stop by my office and we had quite a few heart-to-hearts."

"Was she fearful of her husband?" Mary asked.

"Definitely. Mr. Ramirez would call my office looking for her, and I would say I hadn't seen her. He'd fly off the handle and curse at me over the phone. Truth be told, she came here to get away from everything and everyone. You should talk to Taylor and Christie. They were quite close. Taylor played pro ball for the Padres, as you know, but he wasn't at all like Angel."

"What do you mean?" Mary asked.

"Angel thought everyone was beneath him simply because he played baseball—especially Kate. I know he thought of me as the hired help. Taylor, on the other hand, has shown me nothing but respect. Anyway, I'm rambling. Let me know if you need anything. I'll be in my office. It's up by the Marlin Club. You got a key to the boat?" Les asked, sounding like he might have a spare set in his office.

"Yes," Mary said, holding up the keys.

"What a shame. What a goddamn shame. Kate was…" Les said as he choked up and walked away.

Being familiar with the slips, Mary found the Sea Ray easily and stepped onto the swim step. The big boat was beautiful but also had obvious signs of neglect. The canvas was covered with bird droppings and the hull had so much growth on it the sea grass looked like a hula skirt swaying in and out with the surge. Before unlocking the salon door, Mary put on latex gloves to preserve any additional evidence she might find. After stepping inside, she scanned the interior, thinking this had to be one of the nicest boats she had ever been on. The tan interior, cherry wood accents, and faux granite counters in the galley gave the boat a very rich look. Mary assumed it was Kate who had tastefully added accents like throw pillows, flowers, and other touches to make the boat seem quite cozy. Wow. She could easily live aboard this boat. It was practically bigger than her downtown condo—and nicer, too. Looking around, she noticed a wireless router on a shelf next to one of the three flat-screen televisions. She started searching for a computer. There wasn't a desktop model anywhere, so she figured it must be a laptop. She pulled out a folder and looked at the long catalog of evidence. No laptop was listed. Mary carefully searched all the nooks and crannies of the boat and discovered two things. One, boats have all sorts of interesting and clever places to stow things. And two, Kate did indeed spend a lot of time here; there were enough clothes, shoes, and grooming supplies to last a month. This looked less like a boat and more like a second home. Mary didn't know what she was looking for exactly, but she hoped to stumble upon something that would yield a new line of investigation—to solidify the case against Angel, find Kate's body, or ideally, both. As Mary mulled over her next move, she heard the slider open above.

"Mr. David, is that you?"

Mary made her way up the stairs and was startled to see a man moving toward her very quickly. That was the last thing she would be able to remember because he kicked her hard in the forehead.

❊ ❊ ❊

When Mary woke up it was dark. She must have fallen back down the stairs and hit her head because it throbbed in front and in back. She slowly got up to a sitting position and opened the refrigerator to her right and pulled out an ice-cold bottle of white wine. She then put the wine to the bump on her forehead and passed out.

❈ ❈ ❈

"Mary, what are you doing down there? Mary?"

"What? Christie, is that you?" Mary's words were a little sluggish, as she came to.

"It's me. I bumped into Les the dock guy, and he told me you were here. I was hoping to catch you before you left. Jesus, you have a huge bruise on your forehead!"

Mary reached up and felt it. She handed Christie the bottle of wine, now warm.

"Did you get drunk, pass out, and hit your head?"

"Puleeze. I was attacked," Mary said.

"What do you mean attacked? By Angel?!"

"No, Angel should still be in jail—I don't think he's making bail. This guy was Hispanic, but it wasn't Angel. It happened so fast. I didn't get a good look at him." Mary had heard victims and witnesses say that same thing so many times that it sounded cliché. She wasn't sure she could even describe the man beyond "Hispanic." Her head throbbed and she had a metallic taste in her mouth. She had never been knocked unconscious before, but she felt nauseous and dizzy and was sweating profusely, even though it wasn't that hot. She tried to stand but couldn't get up without wanting to vomit. Was she followed? Who would want to harm her? It hurt to think.

"Mary, maybe we should call an ambulance. You don't look so great," Christie said as she gave her bottled water.

"I'll be fine. Just give me a minute," she said less than convincingly.

Christie helped her up onto the bed in the forward berth, then got some ice from the boat's freezer and wrapped it in a washcloth.

"What are you doing down here anyway, and why are you wearing surgical gloves?" Christie asked as she gently placed the ice pack on Mary's head.

"I'm prosecuting Angel and I wanted to follow up on the crime scene investigators' report," Mary said and then paused to let the pain in her head subside. "Kate spent a lot of time here, right?"

"Well, Angel may have owned the boat, but Kate was the one who used it. She was down here all the time," Christie said, examining the swelling on Mary's head.

"Doing what?" Mary asked as she slowly got up to sitting position.

"She was writing a novel," Christie said as she gently pushed her friend back down on the bed.

"Do you know if she wrote on a laptop computer?" Mary asked.

"Yeah. As a matter of fact, she left hers on my boat before she…"

Mary sat up again, still feeling the effects of the blow to the head, but her curiosity was piqued. "Were you two close?"

"I guess. I was helping edit her novel," Christie said. "She was on my boat and we were going over a few things, like some plot stuff and characters. She accidentally left the laptop there and that was the last I saw her."

Mary didn't recall seeing anything about Kate's laptop in the case file. "Did anyone from the police or my office get that computer?"

"Yeah. An investigator. But I don't remember his name."

"That's okay—I can find out. What's the book about?"

"It's really weird how close her book is to what happened. It's about a wife whose husband is a professional athlete who abuses her physically and emotionally. Only, in her book, her main character escapes before he has a chance to kill her."

"Interesting. I'd really like to read it," Mary said.

"Sure. I don't see why not—I'll email it to you. Kate had sent a copy to a literary agent she'd met at a writers conference, but hadn't heard anything since. That's when she asked for my help. But truth be told, the book is pretty damn good just the way it is."

"So, why did she come to *you* with her manuscript?" Mary asked.

"I see you have your tact—or I should say, lack of tact—back. Feeling better?"

"I'm sorry. I forgot you were a teacher. You're a P.E. teacher, right?" Mary asked with a wink.

"Funny. I think Kate felt that since I was married to an ex-ballplayer I would have some insight into what her character was going through. But you know Taylor, he's nothing like Angel—even when he played for the Padres. Angel… he's a real shithead, you know that. I'm glad you're the one prosecuting him, Mary. I hope you nail his ass to the wall for what he did."

"Gladly, but it'll be a tricky case—there's no body."

"All I know is, Angel was violent. Kate would wear dark glasses all the time. When I called her on it, she showed me her black eye and bruises on her arms. He beat her, Mary, all the time. It's not hard to believe he killed her."

CHAPTER 12

"What are you looking at?" Angel asked an inmate who was staring at him. Angel was in the middle of a call on another inmate's disposible phone. These phones had become the most popular contraband besides drugs and weapons, since calls on them were hard to trace back to anyone.

The inmate just shook his head and said, "You look sorta familiar, like I've seen you on TV or something."

A larger inmate nearby grabbed the guy by the shirt and said, "That's Angel Ramirez. He plays for the Padres. Now stop staring and give the man some room."

"Angel Ramirez, really? Man, that's cool. Hey, Angel…"

That's all the guy could get out before he was taken down and had his head slammed on the floor. "You do not address Angel directly, got that?" The inmate couldn't respond since he was unconscious, but he got the message just the same.

"What's going on there?" Manuel, the private investigator asked on the other end of the phone when he overheard the ruckus in the background.

"It's nothing. So, what did you find out?" Angel asked.

"Well, I've got some good news and some bad news. The good news is I think I have an idea where Kate might be," Manuel said.

"Yeah. What's the bad news?" Angel asked.

"When I went down to your boat there was a woman there poking around," Manuel said.

"Did you, uh, take care of her?" Angel asked, glancing around to make sure he wasn't overheard. After the earlier altercation, the other inmates gave him plenty of space.

"In a manner of speaking," Manuel replied.

"So, where is the bitch hiding?" Angel said loudly, not caring if anyone overheard it.

"I can't tell you precisely, but I found a computer disc on the boat that contained what looks like a rough draft for a book and her research notes," Manuel said.

"What are you talking about?" Angel spit out.

"You didn't know your wife was a writer?" Manuel asked.

"Kate? Come on. No way. All she could write was checks—lots of them."

"Well, that's what it looks like to me. I read it and it's basically a blueprint on how to change your identity and disappear," Manuel said, clearly impressed by Kate's research on the subject.

"She left all this behind?" Angel asked, surprised because of Kate's usual attention to detail.

"She must have forgot she put the computer disc with the music discs, but there it was. I don't know why the cops missed it. The reason I took it was because it said 'Angel' on it. I spent some time looking over her notes and the rough draft of her book and I think I know how she was able to pull it off."

"Fuck. I can't believe it. Where did the she get the money to run?"

"Did you ever give her diamond earrings?" Manuel asked.

"Yeah, so?"

"Well, what I think she did was pawn them along with her diamond ring and replace them with fakes," Manuel said as he flipped through his pocket note pad.

"*Mierda!* What else did the *puta* do?" Angel asked, surprised by his wife's cleverness.

"According to her book, I think she was siphoning off money from your household expenses and stashing it away."

"How much, Manny?"

"It's hard to say. Could've been tens of thousands." Only silence came through the phone. "Angel?"

"I'm here. What else?"

"In her notes was a lot of details about how to build a new identity. Do you know a guy named Robby Gomez?"

"Yeah, he lives a couple of doors down from me."

"Do you know what Robby does for a living?"

"No," Angel said softly.

"He owns a little photo-processing place on Palm Avenue. I know you've seen it. The place is a dump. So how does he afford to live on the same block as a big spender like you?"

"What's he, a drug dealer?" Angel asked.

"Nope. I asked around and found out he's the

guy you go to when you need a driver's license, pass-
port, birth certificate, or a social security card. And
these aren't fakes, either. He's got a source who can
hack into the DMV's computer and other government
computers. He can even create a whole credit history
for you with the three reporting agencies—and it all
looks legit."

"No shit."

"Yeah, but it don't come cheap. I heard he charges
$5,000 each for the driver's license and passport and
another $5,000 each for the birth certificate and social
security card," Manuel reported.

"She could've met our friend Robby when she was
out getting the mail or taking out the trash," Angel said.
"Who knows, maybe he was screwing her when I was
out of town. I want him killed. But first, torture that bastard until you get her new name and where she's hiding.
I also want to know if he was sleeping with my wife.
You got that, Manny?"

"Calm down, Angel. You don't take out a guy like
Robby without some serious repercussions, if you know
what I mean. Besides, I think I know where Kate is. It
seems she had a particular interest in Kauai," Manuel
said.

"Kauai? I'm fucking stuck in this shithole, my career ruined, and that bitch is lying on some beach on
Kauai."

"I take it you want me to book a flight there right
away?" Manuel said.

"You're damn right I do."

"Okay. I'm going to have someone slip you a

phone, so you don't have to use that other guy's, and I'll call you when I get there."

"Do that."

CHAPTER 13

Sandi ripped open the FedEx package and stared at the cover of the advance copy of *Angel* and said into the phone, "Thomas, this is amazing," On the cover was a woman looking a lot like Jackie O with a wide-brim hat and sunglasses staring off into the distance with the slightest "Mona Lisa smile" forming on her lips. "You're a genius. How did you get it into production so soon?"

"When I stood up at the editorial meeting and told my colleagues that the missing wife of baseball star Angel Ramirez had written a book before she disappeared, their mouths dropped to the floor. They were speechless—except for the sales and marketing people. They couldn't contain themselves. They know how much media attention has been focused on this woman, and now she has a book. What they said was, 'A dying woman's last words as she predicts her own demise in a novel based on true events. You've seen her face on the news, now learn the rest of the story.' I have never seen so much excitement surrounding a first-time author. And when I told them the book was gripping and extremely well written, well, they didn't care, but that's beside the point." The editor chuckled at his own joke.

"So where are we now, Thomas?" Sandi asked sweetly.

"As soon as you approve the bound galleys, we can go to press."

"Done," Sandi said, knowing full well this was usually the part of the publishing process where the author pours over the manuscript scrutinizing every word, an exhaustive and time-consuming proposition. Sandi couldn't care less about the content. She wanted the book on bookstore shelves as soon as possible.

"Okay, then. Since you're handling the role of spokesperson for the book and will be doing all the media, I want you to talk to our PR person. We'll leak the news to the media that this book exists and I have a feeling they will do the rest. Pack your bags, Sandi, you're going to be on a book tour by the end of the month."

"Have the salespeople contacted the chains about preorders?" Sandi asked.

"Let's just say we have already pre-sold the first printing and half of the second," Thomas McGunne said proudly, all his worries about the book behind him. He now had no regrets about buying the rights to the manuscript or the price he paid.

Sandi grabbed a calculator off her desk and began figuring out what that meant in royalties. Not bad she thought, but a drop in the bucket compared to what she would get from optioning the book to Hollywood and selling the paperback rights.

"By the way, I was wondering, you don't happen to have any more manuscripts by Ms. Ramirez, do you?" Thomas McGunne asked.

"The next book will demand a much bigger advance than the first one did, that's for sure. Why, interested?" Sandi asked.

"Come on, greed doesn't become you. On second thought, it actually does suit you perfectly," McGunne said. "So, do you have another title to sell?"

"I'm sorry, Thomas, that's the only manuscript I know of. If I do discover another one, you'll be the first to know."

"I hope so," he said.

CHAPTER 14

Kate had established herself in Wiamea, her red Jeep a familiar sight for the locals in front of the market, movie theater, and all the best beaches. Her routine of going for a morning swim at Salt Pond Beach Park, then a stop for coffee at Grinds on the way home, followed by a run along the beach in the afternoon seemed dangerous. She worried it could be her downfall. Lately, Kate rarely left the west side of the island. If that creepy singer from San Diego asked around, he wouldn't have much trouble finding her. Kate decided to change things up a little, driving through Waimea and then veering off the main road toward the historic town of Hanapepe. The tiny town was bustling with tourists and there were several other red Jeeps just like hers parked nearby. As she wandered the historic town she saw a sign for the Talk Story Bookstore and Café. The Plantation Inn had a lending library of books that had served her well considering the cottages didn't have televisions. Still, a bookstore held much allure. As an aspiring writer, Kate had spent much of her time back in San Diego staring at the books on the shelves wondering what it would take to get hers there, too. She crossed the street and walked into the store, a small independent that seemed to specialize in used books. There was a circle of chairs in the corner and quite a few people milling around. Kate went to the reference section and pulled down an old copy of Literary Marketplace and began searching through the section of agents. Maybe she would write again under a surname. She would need a new agent, since her current one didn't seem to know or care that she existed. Ms. Golding gladly took her money and proceeded to do absolutely nothing—not even return her calls or respond to her letters.

"Agents," a voice from behind said sarcastically.

Kate spun around thinking it was Bob. It was an older man in glasses, his long graying hair pulled back into a ponytail, clearly taken aback by her reaction. "I see you know what I mean. Have you heard the one about the author who died and in his will included the provision that fifteen percent of his ashes be thrown in the face of his agent?"

Kate couldn't help but laugh and said, "I would be happy to have fifteen percent of my advance go to an agent. That would mean my book was published."

The man nodded and smiled in an understanding way. "I take it you're a writer."

"Well, a wannabe, I guess. I've never been published."

"My name is Edward, and this is my store."

"Wow, I'm impressed. Are you also a writer?"

"Me, oh no. I'm a fan and follower of writers, but I have never been able to do it myself."

"I'm starting to wonder if I have what it takes, too," Kate said as she returned the big book to its space on the shelf.

"You know, we have a writers group that meets here once a week. You should sit in on a meeting."

"I don't know. When's your next meeting?" Kate asked.

"In about five minutes."

"Oh. Well, I guess I can fit it into my busy schedule," Kate said and then laughed at her own joke.

Edward laughed loudly, too, and steered her toward the area of the store where the chairs were set up in a semi-circle. Several people stood around. He started to introduce her: "This is, oh, I didn't get your name."

"Kay," Kate replied quickly.

"Kay is going to sit in with the group."

Introductions were made and everyone eventually sat down, waiting for Edward to begin, which he did right away. "We are the Westside Writers Group…"

"I thought we were going to call ourselves The Future Best Sellers Of America," said Chris, the editor of the local newspaper and author of a popular guide to the island.

"How about we make that the subtitle?" Edward suggested and everyone laughed. "This meeting, I thought we would do something different. I think you'll like this, Chris. I took a look at the *New York Times* best seller list to get an idea of what's hot and ordered copies of each title." He pointed at a pile of new books in a box next to him on the floor. "Of course I'll return them to the wholesaler as soon as we're done." Again the group laughed. "But before we begin I'd like to learn a little more about our guest and her ambitions as a writer.

What do you say?"

The group cheered enthusiastically.

As much as Kate wanted to bolt for the door, she welcomed the chance to talk about the craft of writing, as well as the frustrating trials and tribulations of the publishing business, with people who would understand. She never even mentioned to Angel that she was writing a book. He would have told her she was too stupid to write anything worthwhile. Christie, her friend from the marina, was the only person who had read what she had written, and she was always encouraging while making suggestions about how to improve her book.

"Kay, the floor is yours. Tell us what you write, want to write, and where you are now with your writing."

Kate's throat was suddenly dry and her hands started shaking. She wondered what she could say without giving away too much. She stood and decided to share the parts of her story that were safe to tell.

"I've always wanted to be a novelist," Kate began. She went on to tell the group about her writing ambitions, the agonizing struggle of writing her first work of fiction, and the frustration she had with her agent. The more she spoke, the more she wanted to speak. It felt good to talk about her literary dreams. She'd forgotten how much she wanted to be published. When she was done, the audience peppered her with questions.

"How did you get your agent?" one woman asked.

"I met her at a writers conference," Kate said with a healthy dose of distaste. "But—"

"What's her name?" a man interrupted, pen and

paper in hand, ready to write her name down, even though Kate clearly was not pleased with her.

"After all the negative things I've said about her, I'd rather not reveal her name."

"What's your novel about?" Edward asked.

This was the question Kate was dreading. "It's a story of hope and rebirth," was what she came up with for a safe answer.

"Part of what this group does is read and critique, if you're interested," Edward said.

"Really? That's great," Kate said forgetting for a moment the implications of anyone reading what she had written. Then it hit her like a ton of bricks. Her manuscript was out there. Her agent had a copy. Christie had a copy and… Oh my God, Christie had her laptop. After all of her careful planning, how stupid to leave her laptop behind—with the manuscript right there. Kate tried to recall what she had written in the pages of her novel. Would someone be able to piece together where she went based on her book? Her character, much the same as Kate had done in real life, created a new fake identity complete with a driver's license and credit cards and escaped to a tropical island to begin her new life as a completely different person. Clearly, it was too close for comfort.

After everyone finished asking Kate their questions, Edward passed the best-selling books around. Kate absentmindedly took one and put it on her lap. She was lost in thought, retracing the steps she took to disappear and mentally comparing them to her manuscript. Kate relaxed a little when she remembered that her work was probably in a slush pile somewhere in her agent's office and Christie had probably stopped editing the book when she hadn't heard from Kate over the past few weeks. She didn't dare contact anyone on the mainland for fear that it might somehow get back to Angel, and he would certainly come looking for her. Kate looked at the book on her lap, a copy of J.K. Rowling's *Harry Potter And The Deathly Hallows*. She picked up the tome and smiled. She secretly loved the Harry Potter books and had read the entire series except for this newest installment.

"Okay, you all have your best-sellers. Now let's have a look at what made these books so successful. Jenny, why don't you go first? What do you have and why do you think it made the list?"

Jenny, a scholarly looking young haole woman, wrapped her dark hair around her ears, pushed her glasses back, and started to explain why her pick was a best-seller. "It's clear why this book made the list. The author was killed by her famous husband before the book was published."

"So what you're saying is, dying a violent death will increase your chances of getting a book deal," Edward interjected.

Everyone laughed, including Kate.

"No, but you know what they say, any publicity is good publicity. All the news channels have covered the woman's story ad nauseam. The search for the body, the famous baseball player's denial he did it, and so on."

That caught Kate's attention who had been preoccupied reading the dust jacket of the Harry Potter book.

Someone said, "I don't watch the news. What happened to the author?"

"Her husband, Angel something or other, repeatedly abused her," Jenny said. "Then one night he beat her to death and disposed of her body because nobody's seen her since. Apparently, she was writing about the abuse because her book is so much like her real-life story, except that the protagonist escapes to a tropical island with a new identity and a new life."

Kate tried to speak but her throat was too dry. Finally she squeaked out her question, "What's the author's name?"

The young woman looked down at the cover and said, "Kate Ramirez".

Kate's mind was racing in a million different directions at once. Everyone thought she was dead and that Angel did it. How perfect is that! Okay, it wasn't perfect. She couldn't let Angel be convicted for a murder he didn't commit. Or could she? Did she have a choice? If she went back to clear his name, he would absolutely kill her for real when he was released. And didn't he essentially kill her years ago when he turned her into a trophy wife and personal punching bag? On the other hand, her stepsister and niece would think she was dead. That wasn't fair to them. They weren't close, but to believe someone from your family was murdered was terrible. Then there was the anger—at herself. How could she be so stupid and leave a book behind that would ultimately lead Angel right to where she was hiding? Knowing he didn't kill her, he would certainly send someone to find her, and her book would lead the hitman here eventually. Strangely, she was also excited. Her book had become a best-seller. This was not how she imagined it would happen, but it still felt great all the same. This is what she had always wanted. To write books and have them read by as many people as possible and now it was happening. If she went back to the mainland, she would do so as a bestselling author and the truth about Angel would be out there. But so would Angel and chances are, he would kill her for real.

Kate's brand-new book had been passed around until it reached her. As she held it in her hands and the others carried on a conversation that turned their attention from her, the emotions she was feeling were so powerful she started to cry. Tears ran down her cheeks as she stared at the cover and then her photo on the back. That seemed so long ago. She was a much different person now. Wiping away her tears, Kate opened the book and saw the publisher was Gladstone Books, a prestigious publishing house by all accounts. Then a thought occurred to her. Who submitted her book to Gladstone? Was it Christie? Unlikely. Kate opened the book to the acknowledgment page and read the list of people "she" had thanked, none of whom she knew. The most glowing thank-you was to her agent, Sandi Golding. Wait a minute. If this book is a best-seller, then who gets the money? Angel? Oh God, no. Wait a minute, she thought, Angel is being accused of killing her. There is no way he would get the money. Oh, no. The agent is probably the one getting rich from this book. Her book. Kate didn't care as much about the money as she should have, but the thought that it was all going to her agent was too much to take. Kate opened her novel and began to read her own words in print. The feeling was overwhelming. She felt giddy, like it was her birthday and Christmas morning all in one. She couldn't wait to go back to her cottage and read the rest.

"Miss, it's your turn," the woman seated next to her said as she tapped her on the shoulder.

"Oh, I'm sorry, I have a lot on my mind," she said, realizing at that moment as she stared down at her own book that she was now in an elite group—authors with a book on the best-seller list. She had a renewed confidence. "Before I tell you about *Harry Potter*, I was wondering, where on the best-seller list is this book?" she asked, holding up her own novel.

Edward glanced at the list and said, "Number one in its first week. Pretty impressive."

Kate fought to keep from grinning ear to ear. "Number one, wow!" Then, to not draw too much attention to her book, she also asked, "And *Harry Potter*?"

"Uh, number six. Yes, sixth."

"Well, I think the reason J.K. Rowling's books are so successful," Kate began, "is that she is a master storyteller with a large and loyal following and brand that has been built through word-of-mouth marketing and mass marketing. In effect, she has done everything right."

The group started discussing the Harry Potter series while Kate quietly gathered her things and walked over to Edward. "This was the best thing for me at this time," she said. "I can't thank you enough for including me, but I've got to run—busy schedule and all."

"It was my pleasure. I hope you'll come back," Edward said smiling at her joke.

"I will. And I'd like to buy these two books." Kate handed him a fifty dollar bill. "Keep the change," she said bouncing out of Talk Story Bookstore clutching her new novel. She was now a bestselling author and nothing could ruin this feeling—nothing.

CHAPTER 15

Bob Sommers sat on his ratty couch watching the *To-day* show wearing the same black Grateful Dead concert tee and baggy shorts he'd worn the day before, and the day before, and the day before that. His filthy feet rested on the coffee table, his guitar sat listlessly in his lap, and of course, Bob had a beer in his hand. With his first beer finished before breakfast, he reluctantly got up off the couch because another was in order, but the small fridge in his tiny apartment was empty. Slamming the door to the fridge in frustration, he was a beaten man. No money, no hope, no future, and worse than all that, no beer. He just couldn't catch a break. His wife left him for another man almost a year ago while he was on the road with his band playing small clubs across the country—nailing anything and everything that came his way. After a tiny taste of success, his music career was now going nowhere. The small record label that released his debut CD folded—in part because of the lackluster sales from his own failed effort. This meant his CD was out of print and he was out of luck—and money. Actually, he was worse than broke. He owed the wrong people a few thousand dollars—plus interest—money he borrowed to finance his last tour, which failed to sell out even one date. The reason he came to Kauai was to avoid being beaten to a pulp (or worse) by the loan shark who fronted him the cash to travel and play the club circuit. Between the gig at the Brewery two nights a week and a night at Whaler's, he could barely pay the rent. He needed a miracle. Instead of praying, he took a hit off the bong that was as much a part of the décor as his empty beer can collection. Then his prayers were answered. Being interviewed by Matt Lauer was a short, heavyset woman named Sandi Golding. The agent was blabbing on about a bestselling book she "discovered" written by Kate Ramirez, the dead wife of Angel Ramirez. When they showed the late author's picture on the screen, Bob knew exactly what to do.

❈ ❈ ❈

Instead of swimming laps in the calm waters of the protected cove as she did each and every morning, Kate just floated there on her back, giggling and giddy one minute, panic stricken and pained the next. She was a published, bestselling author living in paradise. It didn't matter to her that nobody would ever know the truth; she was overwhelmed with joy because she had done it. Her novel was being bought and read by people all across the country. She saw what fame and fortune can do to a person and she was happy with her life exactly the way it was. Knowing Angel was in jail for allegedly killing her meant she was safe for now. Kate knew the right thing to do was to let someone know she was alive and that Angel wasn't a murderer, but Kate believed that the justice system would right the wrong and Angel would be found not guilty by a jury and freed. His career over, money gone and reputation tarnished—exactly what he deserved for the years of abuse she had endured over the years. Her book would be the best revenge of all. Now everyone would know what a louse he really was. Staring at a cloudless sky, blue beyond belief, Kate couldn't help but wonder how much money the book was generating and where it would go in the future. If Angel were found not guilty, he would be entitled to the royalties. The thought made her shiver, even in the 82-degree water. She had to figure out a way to remain in hiding and somehow keep the money from her slimy agent and even slimier husband. When she was being beaten by Angel and needed a way out, she wrote. That's what she did best—write. Now it was time to write a new chapter in the drama that is her life. She had the beginnings of an idea and was working it out in her head when someone called her name from the beach—her real name.

"Katherine!"

Kate knew better than to look, so she tried to recognize the voice. It sounded familiar, but she couldn't place it. The fact that someone, anyone was calling her by her given name made her stomach turn, but she could not look or else it was over.

"Kate, it's me, Bob. Get out of the water, we need to talk," he yelled from the sand.

Kate remained floating on her back but took a quick peek and saw Bob standing alone at the water's edge waiting for her to answer. She didn't want to give in that easily. She couldn't.

Kate decided this little turd was not going to ruin her new life and shouted back, "Bob, I told you already, I'm not who you think I am."

"Really. Do you think I'm that stupid?"

"Yes. Yes I do, Bob. Now leave me alone."

"Okay, but don't say I didn't try to make a deal with you before going to the press and telling them who you really are."

"Damn it," Kate said to herself before making the short swim to shore.

CHAPTER 16

For the past two weeks, all Mary could think about was Kate Ramirez. The problem was, the more time she spent looking at the evidence and reading Kate's manuscript, the more convinced Mary became that Kate was alive, just like the protagonist in her novel. The woman had done it. She had escaped to somewhere warm and tropical and was starting her life over. Mary thought of herself disappearing to a place where her boss and co-workers couldn't find her, and it was extremely appealing. She pictured taking longs walks on the beach without a care in the world. No more living for her career, a career she wasn't that thrilled with and was getting more stressful by the day. Her caseload kept increasing, meaning her days off dwindled. She too often worked 12 to 16 hours a day, six days a week, and hadn't had a vacation in four years. Sometimes she felt like nobody appreciated how hard she worked and how much she sacrificed to maintain her amazing success rate at getting convictions in court and hammering out plea bargains favorable to the people of San Diego.

Sadly, the more successful she was in her career, the more her personal life suffered. The thought of running away became more and more appealing. The problem was, that wasn't her style. Plus, her parents would freak out if she quit her job and ran away. It was their dream that she'd be a lawyer, and here she was, the youngest Deputy District Attorney at her level in one of the largest D.A.'s offices in the nation. They'd pushed her into law school and all but sent her application to the district attorney's office when she passed the bar—on her first try. Besides, she was far too pragmatic to just leave everything behind and take off for places unknown. She had a cat for Christ's sake. She had cases pending and people that depended on her. What if she could combine doing her job and escaping for a little while? This made more sense in her Capricorn mind. A vacation was frivolous, but a trip to find out the truth of what happened to a victim in a vicious crime, now that was something she could get behind—and so could her parents. She would have to sell the idea to her boss, but the D.A. owed her a big favor and this was just the way to redeem that.

Mary's mind was spinning with possibilities. Even if she had to take some personal time to pursue this, it was okay with her. She had accrued over two months of paid vacation. Feeling the euphoria of a possible working vacation somewhere far, far away from her crowded office and the stress that went with it, she was imbued with relief. Her first goal was to figure out exactly where Kate had disappeared too. The computer technician in forensics was able to retrieve a lot of data from Kate's laptop and the clues all pointed to the Hawaiian Islands, a place Mary had never been but would love to see. Forensics was also able to uncover a possible alias Kate was now using based on some of the information that had been deleted but was still burned on the hard drive. This newfound information would have to be shared with the defense eventually, except that Angel was without representation at this time so Mary could get away with keeping it to herself for now. Of course she would have to investigate these theories herself before disclosing them under discovery. Mary picked up the phone and made a call that would put her on a path to paradise.

CHAPTER 17

After another grueling week of working for Sandi Golding, Carol, the agent's assistant, needed a break. She sat on the couch in her tiny apartment absentmindedly petting her cat Austen—named after Jane Austen—watching the interesting lives of others featured on *Entertainment Tonight*. To her surprise they were doing a story about the disappearance of bestselling author Kate Ramirez. Carol was transfixed as the "news" magazine show hyped the upcoming story. Carol put on her glasses and put down the manuscript she was reading. She figured if her boss wasn't going to read or represent any of the aspiring authors whose manuscripts were languishing in the slush pile, she would start reading them and hopefully find one worth representing herself—either while working for The Golding Literary Agency or on her own. She didn't know how much more crap she could take from the "great" agent. She was learning a lot, but it was to the point of not being worth the long hours, menial tasks, and verbal abuse. The way Carol figured it, Sandi Golding stood to make over one million dollars from Angel when you included hardback, paperback, foreign, and film rights—and Carol knew that normally the agent gets a 15 percent commission off the top on an advance, royalties, and other rights. Sandi was keeping it all since Kate was dead. As much as that bothered Carol, what really got to her was the fact that this manuscript was in the slush pile all along. If only she had been the one to read it and realize the potential. So now Carol took a manuscript from the slush pile home every night and three on weekends hoping to find the next bestseller. The logistics of how to extradite an author from Sandi when she found that special manuscript was something she had learned from the lady herself. It would be a pleasure to stick it to her using her own tricks. Carol smiled at the thought. The commercial break was over and the show was back on; Carol came back down to earth and watched.

"The new book by bestselling author Kate Ramirez is based on her alleged years of abuse at the hands of her husband, Angel Ramirez—a former major league all-star and currently the catcher for the San Diego Padres. In the book *Angel*, a work of factual fiction, the main character fakes her death and disappears to a tropical island to distance herself from her abusive husband, a professional baseball player. It seems real life is stranger than fiction because the author is nowhere to be found and her real life husband is being held for her murder. Jamie Fowler has the story…"

"Thanks, Fran. There are several questions surrounding the disappearance of author Kate Ramirez. Is it all a publicity stunt to sell books? Was she really murdered by her famous husband? Is she even dead? Or is she in hiding somewhere, very much alive? To get to the bottom of this we caught up with the author's agent,

Sandi Golding, and asked if she thought Kate Ramirez was alive. This is what she had to say…"

Carol frantically tried to find the remote so she could turn the TV up, throwing her cat off the couch in the process. This she had to hear. The show cut to Sandi speaking from a television studio, Carol knew it had to be in Chicago because that's where the agent was at the time, preparing to appear on *Oprah*. The producer at *Entertainment Tonight* must have gone through the publisher to get to Sandi because Carol couldn't remember speaking to anyone from the show. "All I can say is the police and district attorney think she's dead and have enough evidence to hold her husband for her murder. I think it's pretty clear that Kate Ramirez was murdered and her husband did it. Yes, in her book the protagonist escapes from her abusive husband, but that is a work of fiction. It seems that in real life she wasn't so lucky. The plan is to donate a percentage of the proceeds from the book to an organization that helps abused women start over. I know that's what Kate would have wanted."

Give me a break, Carol thought to herself as she listened to her boss lie on national TV. Sandi wouldn't donate a dime to any cause other than herself.

"Others aren't as convinced that this whole thing isn't just a hoax to sell books," *E.T.*'s Jamie Fowler went on, "We talked to people on the street and we got their reaction…" Carol's phone was now ringing.

"Hello, this is Carol," she said as she muted the television.

"I need Tony's phone number."

"Ms. Golding?"

"Carol, I don't have time to play twenty questions. I need Tony Mancuso's number."

"Ms. Golding, I'm at home and his number is at work."

"The minute I go out of town you leave work early. Figures!"

"It's 7:30 at night, on a Friday. I have a life, you know." This was untrue, but Carol felt like it was the thing to say in this situation.

Ignoring Carol's statement, Sandi Golding said, "I need you to go into the office and get me that number and then call me on my cell phone."

"Ms. Golding, I live in Brooklyn. That means I have to take the subway into the city at night, I'm not… Ms. Golding, are you there?" Sandi had hung up before Carol could protest.

❉ ❉ ❉

The media attention the bestselling book was generating had made it all the way to San Diego's jail. Angel rested on the cot in his cell and stared at the ceiling. He had to hand it to his friggin' wife—she played him and he never saw it coming. She'd hit the jackpot. She was now a bestselling author with her own money and a new life, and he was in jail for something he didn't do. Angel smiled because he knew he still had some cards to play and he wasn't ready to fold. He had a plan to not only get his life back, but he'd take hers in the process. The current situation seemed like a disaster, but in reality it was the best thing that could have happened. He would use Kate's newfound fame and fortune against her. Angel swung his legs over the edge of the bed and stood up. He looked out between the bars the best he could, checking both ways to be sure nobody was listening, then pulled out the disposable cell phone he'd bought from another inmate and called his friend on the outside.

"Manny, it's me."

"What's up?"

"Would you be interested in another $25,000?" Angel asked.

"Depends."

"I have an idea about how I can put this whole thing behind me and make money in the process."

"I'm listening."

"If Kate were to die a tragic death in another state while I was incarcerated I would go from being a suspected murderer to a rich grieving husband. I mean, how could I have murdered my wife twice, let alone when I was in here and she was out there? Then, when I am cleared of any wrongdoing and released from jail, I inherit all the money from her book, and I can go back to playing baseball. See what I mean? It's a win-win situation for everyone—except for Kate, of course, but that's the point." Angel grinned from ear to ear.

"$100,000," Manuel said quickly.

"Fine. Make it happen," Angel replied.

"Consider it done," Manuel said and hung up.

CHAPTER 18

"I'd like to talk to Ms. Golding, please," Bob said from a payphone next to the bathroom at Duke's Bar & Grill.

"She's not here. Can I take a message?" said assistant Carol.

"Uh, I really need to talk to her. Do you know when she'll be back?" Bob asked, sounding a little desperate, even though he tried not to.

"She's on the road promoting a book this week. May I ask what this is in regards to?"

"It has to do with the book she's promoting," Bob said before taking a long pull from his beer.

"*Angel*?"

"That's the one. I have some information about the author of that book that I think Ms. Golding will find uh, very, interesting," Bob said while trying not to slur his words.

"I'm her assistant, do you want to tell me and I'll pass it along to her?" Carol said.

"No. I want to talk to Ms. Golding directly. Can you give me her cell phone number?"

"I can't do that Mr…"

"Sommers, Bob Sommers."

"Mr. Sommers. I can give her your number, and

I'm sure she'll get back to you regarding your call."

"Fine. Have her call me at 808-555-2452," Bob said and hung up and walked over to the bar to buy another beer with the money he had extorted from Kate. She'd paid him $2,500 in cash, saying that was all she had. She begged him to keep quiet about what he knew. Ha! As if $2,500 would buy his silence. He should have insisted on sex as part of the deal, but with the way the woman broke down when he threatened to expose her little secret, he didn't think she'd be up for sex—at least not then.

Five minutes later, the pay phone at Duke's rang. Bob ran over to it and out of breath said, "Hello?"

"Is this Mr. Sommers? This is Sandi Golding returning your call."

"Oh, yeah, yeah, this is Bob. I, um, I have some information you might be interested in."

"I'm listening."

"Uh, did you know that the author of the book you're promoting isn't dead?"

"What are you saying, Bob?"

"What I'm saying is Kate Ramirez is alive."

"What makes you say that?"

"I recognized her, and then she told me who she was."

"So you're certain the person you saw is Kate Ramirez?"

"Yup. I recognized her from San Diego."

"Does anyone else know that she's alive?"

"No, not that I know of."

"You haven't told anyone?"

"Nope."

"So why tell me?"

"I saw you on the *Today* show talking about her book and how it's a bestseller and all, and I thought you'd want to know where the author is."

"So tell me," Sandi said.

"Well, I was thinking there should be a reward or something for the information," Bob said, feeling a little out of his league with the fast-talking New Yorker.

"Well, there isn't."

"But if you don't pay me, you'll never find her."

"Bob, come on. Do you think I'm stupid? Your call came from area code 808. That's Hawaii, if I'm correct. You also used your real name, so I can easily find out which of the Hawaiian Islands you live on and thus which island Kate is on."

Bob held the phone away from his ear and mouthed the word "fuck" and swirled the last of his beer. Now what? "You still don't know what name she is using or what she looks like now," Bob said, quite proud of himself.

"Okay. Fine. I'll play your game. So, what are looking to get paid for this information?"

"What are you offering?" Bob surprised himself with his negotiation skills.

"I'll tell you what—if you tell me everything you know and promise not to tell anyone else, and I mean nobody, I will pay you $15,000."

"That's less than I hoped for, but I'll take it," Bob said. He could use the money to buy recording equipment and release his next CD on his own terms and his own label. $15,000 would go a long way to make that happen.

"Not so fast. I am going to send an associate with the money. You'll need to meet with him and take him to where Kate is staying. When he sees that your information is correct and the person you say is Kate Ramirez really is, you get paid. Remember, the deal is you don't tell a soul. Deal?" Sandi said.

"Deal," Bob agreed.

"Okay, now start at the beginning and tell me everything you know."

At this point Bob spilled his guts, not even thinking that he was giving away any leverage he may have had. When he was done the agent told him to sit tight and he would be contacted in a day or two. Bob hung up the phone, satisfied with the deal he'd made and the money he would be getting. Back at the bar, he ordered a shot of the best tequila they had and the steak and lobster dinner. He could afford it now.

CHAPTER 19

For all the research she had done on how to disappear without a trace, she had done a poor job of covering her tracks. How could she be so sloppy? How could she overlook the fact that her disappearance would draw major media attention and implicate Angel? The last thing you want is a lot of people looking for you, but that was her current situation. Then there was the manuscript and laptop she left behind. Both of these in the wrong hands would surely lead anyone who was interested straight to her. Now that her book was being read by tens of thousands of people, someone was sure to figure out what she'd done and come looking for her. Finally, she should have known better than to eat in a place every single night where she may meet someone from the mainland who would recognize her—let alone work there. She should have stayed hidden away in her cottage like she planned. Everything that could wrong had. Now she was on the run, all but broke, and not sure what to do or where to go.

When Kate checked out of her bungalow at the Plantation Inn she tried to make it seem she had planned to leave this week all along. That's when Vina pointed out she had paid for the entire month in advance just a few days earlier, in cash. Vina gave her the pro-rated amount back and asked if everything was okay. Kate said everything was fine, but Vina saw through the charade and offered to help. Not sure where else to turn, Kate told Vina the truth (another mistake—every book she'd read about how to disappear said to trust no one), but it felt really good to get it off her chest. Vina was completely nonjudgmental, supportive even—and helpful. When Vina offered Kate a place to stay for free, she accepted. The owners of the Inn also owned a couple of condos that were empty this time of year and, as a bonus, they were on another side of the island. Nobody would bother her there and she could plot her next move the only way she knew how. She would write about it.

CHAPTER 20

"Honey, I know you want an iPod. So do I, but they're expensive and we just can't afford it. Okay, sweetie?" Amy said as she patted her daughter's head. A single mother, she needed the money for more important things like food.

"But mom, everyone had one at school last year and their parents aren't rich," the seven-year-old said.

"Sweetie, not now, okay. We just don't have the money."

"Hey, Mom, I have an idea. We can charge it," the girl said hopefully.

Amy rolled her eyes and said, "Let's see if your daddy sent any money this month when we get the mail from the box, okay? Then maybe we can get one." Amy knew that getting an iPod was just the start. They would also have to find some way to buy the songs to play on it without having the money or even a computer.

"Really, Mommy. Come on, let's hurry," the little girl said as she pulled her mom along the sidewalk toward the postal place.

Their weekly ritual of going to get the mail usually ended in disappointment. Her deadbeat ex sent her child support sporadically. The fact that the mother and daughter had to have a post office box was reason enough not to expect payment. This was a precaution to make sure her ex didn't exactly know where they lived. He was a scary dude. Since the split, his anger had dissipated some, but the threats he made during the divorce still scared her to the core. What she ever saw in him was a mystery to her. Actually, she knew. She always preferred a "bad boy." Look where that got her. She was now a single mom working two jobs just to pay the bills—barely. It killed her that she was unable to provide for her daughter.

Amy put the key in and opened the box handing the mail to her daughter to sort, as they did every week.

"Hey, Mom, who do you know in Arizona?"

"I don't know. Why?"

"There's a letter here postmarked 'Arizona' with no return address."

Amy looked at the handwriting on the letter and it looked vaguely familiar. She put the letter in the pile of mail to save and asked, "Anything from your father?"

Her daughter just shook her head and dumped the junk mail in the trash.

"I'm sorry, baby. Maybe next week."

Amy looked through the stack of mail and stopped at the letter from Arizona again. Could her ex be sunning himself in Arizona while the two of them froze their asses off every winter in northern New Jersey? She ripped open the envelope, surprised to find $1,000 in hundred-dollar bills enclosed. She quickly unfolded the letter and began to read…

Dear Amy,

It's been too long. I hope this letter finds you well. I am sure by now you have heard about my demise. Obviously, rumors of my death are greatly exaggerated. The truth is, I just couldn't take any more abuse from Angel. I came up with a way to disappear to a place where he would never find me so I could begin a new life. I know you know what I am talking about. You managed to get away from Bruce, and I'm now free from Angel. Unfortunately, things haven't gone exactly as I had planned. I know we haven't been close since I married Angel and moved to the west coast, and I apologize I wasn't there to support you when you needed me most. I haven't been a part of your life and I want to be. I want to get to know my step-niece. I also want to help you if I can. That's why I'm writing. I think there is a way we can help each other. I realize I am being vague and this is a lot to ask, but I just hope that you can forgive and forget the past and we can build back our friendship. I need you do something for me—for us. If you can help me out, I need you to e-mail me at the address below. I get the feeling there are a lot of people looking for me so I can't be too careful. Please promise me you won't tell anyone that I've contacted you and that I'm alive. When you e-mail me I'll explain. If you can't, or don't want to get mixed up in this mess, burn this letter and keep the cash. I'm hoping and praying that you will at least let me know how you are via e-mail and listen to what I have to say. I promise to make it worth your while.

With Love,

Kate

authorontherun@hotmail.com

Amy was stunned. She put the letter back in the envelope and counted out the money. Her daughter saw this and asked, "Mom, is that from Daddy? Does this mean I can get an iPod now?"

Amy tried not to laugh. "No, honey, Daddy didn't send any money," she answered as she restrained herself from saying something snide. "This is from your aunt Kate, and no, it's not for a new iPod." Amy hoped her daughter wouldn't blurt this out later in the presence of others.

"Oh. Who is aunt Kate?"

"Well, technically she's not your real aunt, since we are only stepsisters, but we used to be close until…"

"Until what?"

"I'll tell you all about it when you're older."

"Mom! I hate when you do that."

"Sorry, but it's a long story and right now I've got to get to a computer."

CHAPTER 21

Kate remembered reading somewhere that a famous novelist began all of her books by asking the question "What would happen if…?" and started writing her book based on the answer to that question. Kate sure had a "what if" to work with. She spent her days dividing her time between reading her novel and writing her next one. The feeling of reading her own words now as a hardback bestseller was exhilarating. As best as she could remember, the book was published almost word for word. The publisher had made very few changes. She found that amazing, considering what she had read of other authors' complaints about having their manuscripts ripped apart in the editing process. What should have been a joyous time for an author ended up being both demoralizing and depressing. The suggestions and corrections written in red ink and Post-it Notes with even more notes made this a tedious task. The end result was their books had to be rewritten and changed so much they barely reflected the original manuscript. The confidence from being able to get it right the first time eliminated a lot of the fear she wouldn't be able to write another bestseller. Too bad nobody would read this new one. She just wanted to write the sequel as a way to escape and create a happy ending—for herself. This time she wouldn't be so careless with the manuscript and allow it to get into the hands of people who could use it to locate her again. She'd concluded after reading *Angel* that she had leaked enough information that anyone could easily figure out it out and find her. Not this time.

It took her less than two weeks of writing day and night to finish the sequel to *Angel*. She only left the condo to go into town and purchase groceries—and coffee, lots of coffee. Now that it was done she had to leave the safety and comfort of the condo to take care of a couple of critical tasks. The first thing she had done was find a place with Internet access and set up a Hotmail account. She found the perfect place in Old Koloa town—a coffee shop and Internet café hidden away from the hustle and bustle of tourists. Kate had taken no chances this time, dying her hair red and wearing an Arizona Diamondbacks baseball hat she'd found on the beach. She'd always parked her Jeep off the beaten path and walked into the tiny town. The only risky thing she had done was to ask a tourist to mail a letter for her when they got home. That turned out to be easier than she thought, after flirting with a man from Arizona who liked her hat. Now all she could do was wait for her stepsister to reply. This was a lot like the publishing process: hurry up and wait. But she would keep busy by preparing everything so that when, hopefully, her stepsister did decide to help, all would be ready. And sooner would be better, because after paying that idiot Bob $2,500 and sending $1,000 to Amy, she had very little money left.

CHAPTER 22

Amy read the e-mail again, weighing the meaning of what it implied and wondering whether or not she should do it and if she did, how she would pull it off. Would she be breaking the law if she did what Kate wanted her to do? No, not really, not that it really mattered anyway. There was also the challenge of finding someone who would watch her daughter while she was away. Since it was summer vacation, Jenny wouldn't miss any school. She guessed her mom could watch her for a couple of weeks, but that wouldn't come without strings attached. What about her jobs? It would be next to impossible to find someone to fill in for her for a week. But it wasn't like her jobs were anything she couldn't replace if they didn't grant her the time off. Still, she'd like to keep them if she could.

She also wondered if it would be easy to convince the book agent to pay. Could she pull it off? Too bad the agent wasn't a man, because then for sure she could get him to pay using what she always did to get by—her body. Maybe the bigger question was what was in it for her. How much would Kate give her for pulling this off? Knowing Kate, not much. Kate had always been tight with money, refusing to help her out when she needed it most. Kate claimed she and her husband were not as rich as people thought, but Amy wasn't buying it. Angel was a famous baseball player, for cryin' out loud. Kate always thought she was better than the rest of the family and looked down on them, especially Amy. Other than exchanging Christmas cards, they had maybe talked on the phone three times in the past seven years. Kate didn't even ask her to be in her wedding. Hell, she didn't even invite her. And Kate didn't remember her daughter's birthday—not once. When her stepfather died suddenly, Amy couldn't afford to fly out to California to attend the funeral; she asked Kate to buy her a ticket, but Kate refused, worried that Amy would spend the money on drugs. Now she was sending her $1,000 in cash and asking her to buy a plane ticket to Hawaii— funny how the tables had turned. Now that Kate needed her, Amy wasn't going to let this opportunity pass without getting something out of it. In the subject line of her e-mail back to Kate she wrote, "I'm in"—and she meant it.

When Kate read the e-mail from Amy, she sighed in relief, although the whole plan hinged on her flaky stepsister. Amy was the closest thing to family Kate had left. After Kate's mother passed away, her father met and married Amy's mother a year later. Growing up together, the two had been as close as biological sisters, but grew apart as they got older. While Kate was away at college, Amy got mixed up with the wrong crowd and made a series of poor choices. Her taste in men was dreadful. If a guy told her he was broke, liked to beat women, and had problems with drugs and alcohol,

Amy would say, "Great, let's get married." Some of the guys were truly scary, like Bruce, the man she did marry when she found out she was pregnant with Jenny. Bruce almost made Angel look like, well, an angel. Kate's stepmother insisted she not enable Amy by sending her money, so Kate didn't. This pissed Amy off and she resented Kate for living a seemingly perfect life without her. Putting her future in Amy's hands wasn't an ideal situation, but it had to be this way.

When Kate remembered she had a safe-deposit box in New York from the year Angel played for the Mets, and in this box was an old will, naming Amy as the sole beneficiary of her estate, her plan to get out of this mess started to take shape. Amy was to go to the safe-deposit box and retrieve the document. Since Kate was presumed dead, Amy should be able to get into the box and walk out with the will. Its authenticity and validity could easily be called into question, but for what she needed Amy to do, the outdated will would work fine. Amy had to go to the offices of Sandi Golding and demand a meeting. At this meeting she would present the will and insist the royalties from the book be paid out—immediately. Of course the agent would demand to authenticate the will and stall as long as she could. That's why Amy would ask for a one-time settlement, an amount small enough the agent would grant it without pause. Amy would play the part of the dumb, drugged-out bimbo who lucked into this money and would take whatever she could get. This would not be a stretch for Amy, who could pull it off without even trying. Sandi would seize the opportunity to dispatch this potentially crippling problem for under $50,000. That amount would be enough to help Kate start her new life and leave enough to pay Amy for her troubles—and her silence. After Amy made the deal, she would fly from New York to Kauai and deliver the money. The more she thought about it, the more preposterous it all sounded. So many things had to go just right for this to work and she wasn't going to be there to make sure they did. But as bad as things were, there were a lot of things that had gone right in the past few months, and she was counting on her good luck to continue. It had to.

CHAPTER 23

"Mom, if I could tell you where I was going I would. You know that," Amy said.

Amy's mother gave her a skeptical look.

"Mom, trust me. I'm not running off to get married in Vegas and I'm not using drugs." Two things Amy had done in her recent past.

"Amy, you know I love you. I just worry about you," Amy's mother said while puttering in the kitchen.

"Mom, I'll be fine. Don't worry."

"How will I get hold of you if I need to? If Jenny needs to?" Amy's mom asked while wiping her hands on her apron.

"Mom, you have my cell number. Call me if you need me," Amy said as she pointed to the phone posted on a bulletin board by the phone.

"So you're not leaving the country then?" Amy's mom asked with a raised eyebrow.

"Mom."

"Okay, go. Be careful." She gave Amy an especially long hug and a kiss on her forehead.

"I'm gonna say goodbye to Jenny and then I have to go," Amy said.

"Do you need a ride to the airport, dear?"

"Who said I was flying?" Amy replied and winked.

In the spare bedroom, Jenny was lounging on the bed, listening to her brand-new iPod.

"Jenny, I'm leaving." Nothing.

"JENNY, I'm leaving now."

"Bye, Mom. Say hi to aunt Kate," Jenny said louder than normal. She obviously wasn't used to talking over her new iPod's volume yet. Amy walked over and pulled the small headphones out of her daughter's ears with one quick tug and scowled at her. "What?!" the girl said.

"What do you mean 'what'?" Amy yelled before shifting to a whisper. "Did I or did I not say *not* to mention your aunt's name?"

"Oh, right. Sorry, Mom."

"I mean it. Not a word. Okay?"

"Yeah, okay."

"I'll see you in a week or so. You okay?"

"I'll be fine, Mom."

"Hug?"

The two hugged and Amy headed out of the single-story Paramus home for the red rental car sitting by the curb. She twirled the Hertz key ring on her finger and smiled as she crossed the lawn. Her luck was about to change. Maybe she and Jenny would move out of their cramped apartment and rent a home of their own in the suburbs when she got back. If everything went well, she'd have the money.

❋ ❋ ❋

Amy left the quiet north New Jersey community and headed for the hustle and bustle of New York City. The drive would give her time to go over the plan in her mind, so she'd be ready when she got to the bank. It wouldn't be easy gaining access, but the fact that the box was in Kate's maiden name should make it easier. After getting lost several times, Amy finally found the bank she was looking for in the Flushing area of the city, near Shea Stadium. She parked just outside. Amy sat there, more nervous than she thought she would be. She never felt comfortable around authority figures, and bank employees qualified as authority figures. Amy had an old ID from Kate, one that Kate had taken with her when she escaped Angel, because it had her maiden name on it. Though the two stepsisters looked nothing alike, they believed the plan could work. Amy just had to sell it. She had practiced Kate's old signature until she had it down cold, made herself up to look as much like her stepsister as possible, and studied the information on the ID in case the bank employee asked her a probing question or two. Amy walked into a Starbucks down the block and used the bathroom to change clothes and check her makeup. She was as ready as she would ever be.

※ ※ ※

Amy waited in line at the bank and could swear others could hear her heart beating. Man, she could use a Valium right now to take the edge off.

"Next," the bank teller said without looking up.

Amy was frozen in place.

"Next, please," the teller said, snapping his fingers, locking eyes with Amy, and arching his eyebrows as if to say, *let's go, lady*.

Amy quickly stepped toward the teller with all the confidence she could muster. "I need to get into my safe-deposit box, please."

The teller seemed a little annoyed and said, "Fine, meet me at the end of the counter and have a seat. I'll be right there." He locked up his drawer and walked over to meet her.

"Sign here," he said as he passed her a clipboard with a sign-in sheet. "I'll need to see some ID."

Amy looked down at the signature on the sheet, a perfect forgery. She produced the ID and the teller glanced at it and handed it back. Easy.

"Follow me," he said, and sauntered toward the open bank vault.

Once inside, Amy dropped her purse and gave it an "accidental" kick. Not only was this part of the plan—let the bank guy get a good look at her ample breasts as she bent down to gather her belongings—it would also explain why she couldn't produce a key. But the bank teller's eyes didn't even glance at her cleavage; he didn't swing that way. He did, however, take a second glance at her while shaking his head and tsk-tsking the tackiness of each item she retrieved from the bank floor. The two then made their way to the box, number 31, the same number Angel wore when he was with the Mets.

"Key?" the teller asked with his hands on his hips and a tilt of his head.

Amy made a big production of looking for the key

in her purse before saying, "I can't find the key. It was here when I left my house. It must have fell out when I dropped my purse. Will you please help me look for it?"

The teller blew out some air and rolled his eyes.

"I am so sorry," Amy said as she got down on her hands and knees and began searching."

"Forget it. I can open the box without your key," the teller said as he shrugged at a fellow teller just outside the safe.

He opened the small safe-deposit box and said, "Just holler when you're done. There's a desk over there you can use. While you're doing that, I'll see how much a new key will cost." The teller looked at the registration card and said, "By the way, honey, you paid for five years of box rental when you opened the account, but you're now three months past due. I'll need to collect that when you leave."

The teller spun and walked away and Amy slowly opened the box. Right on top was the will. She glanced at it until she found the part where she would inherit everything upon Kate's death. "Hmmm, who would have thought?" she said to herself. Underneath the will was a manila clasp envelope. Inside were photos of Kate with a black eye and fat lip along with a note that began, *If I should be found dead it is likely my husband, Angel Ramirez, is responsible*. In addition there was a diary that chronicled the abuse from Kate's then-new husband.

"Whoa," Amy said aloud. She'd an envelope with cash in it. Amy couldn't resist counting the bills. $2,750. She wondered if Kate didn't mention the money because she forgot or because she was testing her trustworthiness. Certainly Kate wouldn't object if she used some of the money to pay off the bank. Also in the box were photos of some of Kate's ex-boyfriends. Some of them were torn and taped together and looked like they had been crumpled. She doubted Kate had done anything to the photos. She guessed that Angel had once found the photos and tried to destroy them. There was also a ring and a necklace. Amy put them on and closed the box. After paying the bank for the new key and the fees for the safe-deposit box, Amy left the bank a lot more confident than when she walked in, and with a lot more money.

CHAPTER 23

"Ms. Golding, there is a woman here to see you. She says it's important," Carol announced over the intercom.

"Is she a writer?" Sandi asked, clearly annoyed. Nothing got her going like a pesky and persistent writer who decided to just drop by, thinking Sandi would welcome her with open arms. Yeah, like that would ever happen.

"What is the nature of your business with Ms. Golding?" Carol asked Amy.

"I'd rather not say, but tell Ms. Golding that I am a relative of Kate Ramirez," Amy replied.

Carol raised her eyebrows ever so slightly and an almost imperceptible grin formed on her lips. "Ms. Golding, I think you're going to want to meet with…" Carol put her hand over the mouthpiece of her headset phone and said, "What is your name?" Amy answered and Carol continued, "with Amy."

"Tell her to come back later. I'm busy and quite frankly, I'm tired of this crap. Tell her to come back next week when I'm gone."

"Okay."

"Amy, Ms. Golding said she's too busy to see you today. Can you come back next week?"

"Tell Ms. Golding I am going straight over to meet with the publisher of my stepsister's book and give them what I was going to give to Ms. Golding—the original copy of a will from Kate naming me, her stepsister, as the beneficiary."

"Hang on a second. Let me talk to Ms. Golding. I'll be right back," Carol said.

Carol was loving every minute of this. She knocked on Sandi's door and waited for a reply.

"What?!" the agent barked to her assistant.

"Ms. Golding, may I have a word with you?"

"What is it now? I told you I'm busy."

"Um, I just thought you would want to hear what this woman has to say before she goes to Gladstone to meet with Mr. McGunne."

Sandi opened the door a crack to peek her head out and try to get a look at Amy, now sitting on a corner of Carol's desk and waving at her. "What does she want?"

"She says she can produce a will from the late Mrs. Ramirez naming her as an heir."

Sandi brushed past Carol, hand outstretched, all smiles and full of cheer. "Hi, Amy. I'm Sandi Golding. It's good to meet you."

Amy shook her hand and thought to herself, wow, this lady isn't as much of a bitch as I thought she'd be. Maybe this won't be so hard to pull off after all. "I saw you on TV, Ms. Golding," Amy said before Sandi interrupted her.

"Call me Sandi, please."

Hearing this, Carol rolled her eyes and sat down at her desk.

"Okay, Sandi, I saw you on TV promoting my stepsister's novel and it occurred to me that someone is making a ton of money off the sales of her book. I remembered Kate telling me she had named me in her will, and only me. I have a copy of the will if you'd like to see it," Amy said, digging it out of her purse.

"Come into my office, Amy. I would like to see the will. I didn't know Kate had any family. At least she never mentioned you," Sandi said as she ushered Amy into the expansive office. "That will be all, Carol, and please hold my calls."

"Yes, Ms. Golding."

Amy looked around the room. Framed dust jackets from many of the books Sandi had sold over the years crowded the super agent's office walls. There were also dozens of photos of Ms. Golding posing with celebrities and articles written about Sandi and her success, all mounted prominently. A lot of this was lost on Amy, but she knew enough to be impressed.

"Sit, sit. You brought this will with you?" Sandi asked.

"I did," Amy said as she passed it across the large desk.

Sandi looked it over and said, "It looks like everything is in order. Of course the publisher will want to have their attorneys take a look at it."

"That's why I came to you first. I don't know anything about the book business. I don't even read books, really. I'm too busy. I'm a single mother trying to raise my young daughter."

"I see," Sandi said, not really understanding, since

she'd never had kids. Hell, she didn't even like them.

"What I was hoping for is to come to some sort of agreement, just you and me. I don't want much, but I could really use some cash—in exchange for a copy of the will, of course."

"I don't know, Amy. We really should turn this over to the publisher," Sandi suggested while reading and re-reading the will.

"Like I said, Ms. Golding… I mean, Sandi… I don't want all the hassle and I don't want to wait months or years for the lawyers to figure it all out. I'd rather just give you the will instead."

"I see. And how much money were you looking to get for this will?"

"How much have you made off the book so far?" Amy asked, thinking it was a perfectly reasonable question, not knowing it was totally taboo to talk about money.

"I'm sorry, but that's confidential. But I bet it's less than you think."

"Okay, what would it be worth to you to have the only copy of this will?" Amy asked.

"How do I know it's the only copy?" Sandi replied.

"This was the only one in the safe-deposit box Kate had instructed me to go to in the event she died. As you can see it's the original."

Sandi took another look at the will; it looked like an original all right. Surely the attorney who drafted it had a copy, though. But no one had come forward and they may never make the connection between Katherine Ramirez and Katherine Smith, the name on the will. Regardless, this was leverage and Sandi would use it.

"How do I know the attorney who drafted this isn't going to make a copy of this public?"

"Because he's dead," Amy said. And it was the truth.

"Interesting. Let me just double-check to make sure," Sandi said before hitting the intercom. "Carol, can you please look up and get me on the phone with Mr. Herbert Levy, esquire, here in New York?"

While she waited, Sandi continued to read the will, hoping to find something to prove it was a forgery. Instead, the more she read, the more authentic the document appeared to be. This whole fiasco was turning into a very expensive nightmare. Then Sandi remembered her plans to sell the screen rights for the book and what a windfall that would be. It would likely be a seven-figure deal. She couldn't let this little problem get in the way. As long as the stepsister didn't want a crazy amount, she'd make the deal—and add her to the people on Tony Gravano's hit list just to be sure there would be no more meetings like this. Gravano would do anything she asked if it meant his manuscript would get published. But to make absolutely sure he was motivated enough to knock off Kate and now this greedy little bitch, she would tell Tony his book might be made into a movie.

The intercom buzzed and Sandi pushed a button on the phone. "Ms. Golding, Mr. Levy is, um, he's passed away. I spoke with his widow and…"

"That will be all, Carol."

"Can I see some ID, please?" Sandi asked.

Amy produced her New Jersey driver's license. Sandi looked it over and handed it back.

"I'm willing to offer you $5,000 as a one-time buy-out. Take it or leave it."

"I'll leave it," Amy said as she snatched the will off the desk and headed for the door.

"Wait, wait. Don't be so hasty. This is a negotiation, after all. What are you looking for?"

"$65,000. Take it or leave it," Amy said, mimicking the agent.

"Be reasonable. That is a lot of money, young lady."

"I know you're making a lot more than that off this book. I just want what's fair."

"How about this—I will give you $25,000 now and the rest over the next few months."

"That's a very generous offer, but I need all the money now and I need more than $25,000. I'm sure if I went to the publisher I would stand to make a lot more money, but like I told you before, I just don't want to wait that long."

Sandi pondered this scenario for a second. All of the money coming in would be frozen until this was resolved, if this will surfaced. It could take months. Plus, she would look like a rank amateur for not knowing Kate had a living heir. "Okay, I can write a check right now for $35,000 if you will sign a waiver to all future claims on this estate."

"Sandi, you can have the only copy of this will for $65,000 and I'll sign anything you want."

"I can't do that, Amy. I'm sorry," Sandi said.

"I'm sorry, too."

Amy slowly made her way to the door, put her hand on the doorknob fully expecting the agent to stop her and agree to her terms. But the agent said nothing. Amy opened the door and was feeling an overwhelming sense of loss. She was so close to serious money, but she was now walking away. What was she, crazy? She turned around and said, "How about $50,000?"

Sandi smiled and said, "Who should I make the check out to?"

CHAPTER 24

As the plane banked and headed for the Lihue International Airport, Tony was awestruck by the beauty of the island. The different shades of blue that the water took on were a far cry from the shades of brown Tony was used to seeing back home. The wide empty beaches, lush landscapes, and deep green valleys were all like a dream. Everywhere he looked, Tony saw what could be a picture postcard. For a guy from Jersey, this was paradise. Sure, he was here on business, but there was no reason he couldn't take care of what he needed to and have a little vacation while he was at it. Normally, on arrival, Tony was always first up to grab his carry-on and go. This trip was different. There were scenes of the island on the video screen and Hawaiian music playing in the background. He was in no hurry to do anything—except change out of his city clothes and into a Hawaiian shirt and shorts. He turned to the older couple in the middle and aisle seats and said, "This is my first time to the islands. How about you?"

This was the first thing he'd said to them the whole flight and they politely answered, even though his 280-pound frame and meaty arms had hogged the armrest the entire flight. "Hal and I own a condo in Princeville," the woman said in a nasal, whiny voice that was straining to sound affluent, but came across as annoying instead. "We come here every year for a month or two. We absolutely love it."

"Are there any sights I should see?" Tony asked.

"How long are you here for?" the husband asked as he leaned forward to see Tony past his wife, who was sandwiched between them.

"I'm here on business, but I think I can have it all wrapped up in a day or two. Then I'm on my own time."

"Where are you staying?" the man asked.

In his hurry to get here, Tony had forgotten to book a room. How stupid could he be? "Um, I'm not sure. Where do you recommend?"

"A guy like you," Hal said, "I'd recommend the Marriott. It's right around the corner from the airport."

"Really?" Tony said with a frown.

"Don't let the location fool you. This isn't LaGuardia we're talking about here. The Marriott is right on a big, beautiful bay."

"Thanks," Tony said.

"Oh, here we say *mahalo* instead of thank you," the older woman said as she stood. "Enjoy your stay."

Tony headed straight for the rental cars. He had his mind set on a big Cadillac and that's what he got, along with directions to the Marriott resort, a three-minute drive from the airport. Since he was broke, he put the whole trip on a credit card he'd gotten from a Russian mobster who owed him a favor for a thing he did a couple of months back. The Russian even threw in phony identification because he was so grateful for the work

Tony did. Tony wouldn't be on Kauai long enough for the credit card to be a problem. The cards could be good for between two weeks and two months before the cardholder caught on that someone had opened an account in their name and was charging it to the limit. Identity theft was a booming business for the Russian mob and now that some of the competing crime families were working together, everyone was benefiting.

❊ ❊ ❊

The hotel was beautiful—and big. Tony had the Caddy valet parked and headed for the lobby. With all the exotic Asian art, marble floors, and impressive pillars on the grounds, he felt like a high roller. A giant outrigger canoe carved out of exotic woods hung in the lobby. This place would suit him just fine.

"I'd like a room," Tony said to the beautiful Hawaiian woman working behind the massive granite counter.

"Do you have a reservation?" she asked as she typed away on her computer.

"No, this is a spur-of-the-moment trip," Tony admitted as he stared at the stunning painting hanging on the wall behind the front desk.

"How long will you be staying with us, Mr. Peters?" the Marriott employee asked as she read the name on Tony's phony ID and credit card.

"Hmmm. How about a week?"

"Let's see, I don't have any rooms with an ocean or pool view at this time. We're really busy right now, but

I can put you in a room right off the lobby on the first floor. Will that be okay?"

Tony really wanted to be able to see the ocean, but this made more sense—a room off the beaten path with easy access. "I'll take it," he said, not really concerned with the cost. "Also, I need to get some new shirts, the flowery kind. Where do you recommend?"

"We have several gift shops on the property."

"Perfect. Is there a place I can get a good steak on the island?"

"Sure. We have our own restaurant by the pool and Duke's is at the end of our property. I'll give you a map."

"Did you say Duke's? Is there more than one Duke's on the island?" Tony inquired.

"Not that I know of, and I've lived here my whole life. Here you go. Here's your room key and information packet. Enjoy your stay," Mr. Peters.

"Mahololo," Tony said, trying out the only Hawaiian word he knew, but butchering it.

❅ ❅ ❅

Bob answered the phone on the first ring. He was expecting the call. "Hello."

"Is dis Bob?" Tony asked in his native Jersey tongue.

"Yup. Who's this?"

"I have something you've been expecting, and you have something for me," Tony said.

"Huh?" Bob said through his alcohol-and-marijuana-induced haze.

"I'm a friend of Ms. Golding, numb-nuts."

"Right, right. Sorry, man. I'm a little buzzed right now. Where do you want to meet?"

"Meet me in an hour at Duke's," Tony said.

Dukes? Bob thought. Holy crap. They must have traced his call from the pay phone. How else would they know where he was when he called?

"Okay, Duke's in one hour. You want to meet me at the bar?"

"Yeah, at the bar." Tony said. "I'll be wearing a red aloha shirt."

Bob held back a chuckle and said, "Alright. I'll see you in an hour."

Bob chugged a beer and then headed over to Duke's. It was a three-minute walk from his place and he figured he would get there early and order a few more drinks before the guy got there. This way he'd have him pick up the tab. Pretty smart thinking, Bob thought to himself as he grabbed his keys and headed for the door.

CHAPTER 25

Amy gladly accepted another Jack-and-Coke from the flight attendant. She didn't down the third one as quickly as the first two, but instead put her feet up, sipped her drink, and made herself comfortable in her first-class seat. She had chosen the steak and soon would be dining on filet mignon while watching the movie of her choice on a private screen. This was the life. If she hadn't cashed the check she would have barely had enough money to buy a coach-class ticket, let alone drinks. It was just like her stepsister to leave her with just enough money to rent a car and buy an airline ticket. The $1,000 was long gone, but she looked good. Amy used the $2,750 in the safe-deposit box to stay at the Waldorf Astoria while she waited the required time for the agent's check to clear. The bank wasn't about to hand over $50,000 cash without verification. It gave Amy a chance to go shopping for new clothes and have her hair and nails done. She wanted to look her best when she saw her stepsister. Kate was always so well put together and had all the best of everything while Amy always had that typical Jersey Girl look going on—big hair, lots of makeup, and long nails. She knew she wasn't as hip and stylish as her stepsister, but it was all she could afford. Now that she was going to take $10,000 off the top from the fifty grand the agent paid, she would be able to afford to take a little better care of herself. Another drink arrived along with a hot wet towel to clean up for dinner. She could really get used to going first class.

On the same flight, it so happened that prosecutor Mary sat one row up from the bathrooms in the back of the plane. Hey, she got a great deal on the ticket. She could endure the smell and constant line of people waiting to use the head if it meant she'd get to Kauai and back for under $500. Mary didn't feel comfortable working on her laptop or looking at files with prying eyes everywhere. Instead, she bought a copy of *Angel* (which she would expense) to read on the plane. Although Mary read through the original manuscript, reading the novel again gave her a fresh perspective on things. The more she read, the more the pieces of the puzzle all started to fit. It was all here. Kate had carefully planned the whole escape. Mary wondered if she intended to frame her husband or if that was just a bonus. Mary studied the picture of Kate on the back cover. She had beautiful, long, dark-brown hair, full lips, and stunning green eyes. She looked stylish in every way. What would she look like now? Mary would soon find out.

※ ※ ※

Kate took a big risk picking up her stepsister from the airport, but she felt she needed to be there when Amy arrived. She backed into a space in the first row of the tiny airport's parking lot, just in case she had to leave in a hurry. A ridiculously large sunhat covered her newly dyed red hair, sunglasses hid her green eyes, and loose-fitting shorts and top revealed nothing about her shape. Kate was confident she was unrecognizable and could wait for Amy at the baggage-claim area—less than 100 feet from her Jeep. Kate bought one of the most fragrant flower leis she could find for Amy and stood with the other locals waiting for arrivals from the mainland. A few travelers, mostly tourists, came through the door leading to baggage claim. Kate strained to see, not sure what Amy looked like now, hoping she could recognize her. A flood of passengers came off the plane all at once. Then the amount of people dwindled to just a few and then none. Amy wasn't on the plane. This was so like her—once a flake, always a flake. Maybe she was being too harsh. Something could have happened with the agent, the bank, or the flight. There could be a dozen explanations why her stepsister didn't show. Still, based on her experience, Amy likely just screwed up. That would be more her style. What was she thinking trusting the most *untrustworthy* person she knew with such an important project? Stupid.

"Kate. KATE!" Amy yelled as she strode across the baggage area looking like a million bucks. Kate couldn't believe it. For one, Amy looked nothing like she remembered. Kate had seen her enter the baggage claim area earlier, but didn't think for a moment this was the same person she had last seen several years ago in New Jersey. Oh, but it was. Who else would be so stupid as to yell out her name in a crowd of people?

❋ ❋ ❋

Mary heard someone yell "Kate" and searched the crowd to see who had said it. It was a stylish-looking woman walking towards what looked to be a local. Mary stared at the woman with the hat and glasses whom the other woman had called Kate. Could it be? Mary turned the novel over and compared the two faces. After the two women quickly embraced, they made a beeline for the exit. What if that was Kate Ramirez? Mary decided to leave her checked luggage behind and follow the two women into the parking lot. There was no way she could get a rental car in time to pursue them, so she ran down to departures and grabbed a cab that was dropping off a family of five.

"I know this will sound cliché," Mary said, "but I need you to follow that red Jeep over there, the one leaving the parking lot."

"Hey, it's your money, lady," the cabbie said and sped off.

"Can you stay back a car or two so they don't notice us?" Mary instructed the cab driver. He gave her a funny look and Mary shrugged. "I know I'm being a backseat driver. Sorry." Mary knew she was control freak and had a hard time letting go. Man, she needed a vacation.

"So this is just like in da movies, yeah?" the dark-skinned cab driver said.

"Yeah. Just like in the movies." Mary leaned forward and flashed the cabbie her prosecutor's ID and said, "It is imperative we don't lose that Jeep. Okay?"

"It's a good thing there aren't that many paved roads on the island, yeah? But if dat Jeep goes off-road and gets all freaky, I don't tink I gonna keep up. Yeah?"

"Do your best. This is really, really important," Mary said, and meant it.

What Mary didn't realize is she was being followed, too.

CHAPTER 26

Bob swirled his fourth Coors Lite in a row and set it down on the bar. Out of habit, he looked to where his watch had been on his wrist, before remembering he'd pawned it a couple of weeks earlier.

"Hey 'X', what time you got?" Bob asked Xavier, the bartender.

"Time for you to go, kook," Xavier said, only half kidding.

"Very funny. Seriously, I need to know the time."

"Brah, it's five minutes later than when you asked me the last time," the local-born bartender said, not sure if he should cut this guy off or keep feeding him beers to knock him out for the night.

"What time was that again?"

Xavier rolled his eyes and said, "It's 4:55, music man. You want another beer, brah?"

"Yeah. I'm waiting for a guy in a red aloha shirt. If he comes in looking for me, tell him I went to take a piss, okay?"

"Yeah, sure. Whatevahs," Xavier said and pulled out another Coors Light.

Bob slid off the bar stool and headed for the bathrooms around the corner. When he got back a fresh beer was waiting for him.

"Try look," Xavier said to Bob.

"Huh?"

"I tink your friend with the red shirt just sat down, ovah there," Xavier said as he subtly motioned over Bob's shoulder to a large man sitting alone at a table overlooking the water.

"Transfer my tab, X," Bob said as he grabbed his beer and approached the mainlander who was sipping a soda.

"Are you Tony?" Bob asked as he approached the table, beer in hand.

"You must be Bob," the man said, not bothering to get up or shake his hand. "Have a seat." Tony slid out a chair with his foot.

"Thanks."

"So, how far is it to the place where our mutual friend is staying?"

"From here, it's about a 45-minute drive."

The big man took a sip from his soda and said, "Let's go."

"Now? Don't you want a drink or two first?"

"I'm kinda in a hurry, so let's go. I got a car out front," Tony said, as he stood and pulled the other chair out so Bob had to stand, too.

"Hey, can you at least take care of my tab?" Xavier came over and handed Bob his bill.

"No."

"No. That's it?"

"Okay, *hell* no. Look, Bob, for all I know you're jerking me around. Until I see our friend, I'm not giving you a dime. Come on, pay up and let's go."

Bob peeled off two twenties and left them on the table before following Tony out to his big, four-door sedan. Tony unlocked the doors with the remote and the two climbed in. Bob was getting a little uncomfortable. He hadn't really thought this through. What if Kate wasn't at the Inn when they got there? He hadn't actually seen her in a while. This guy didn't look to be the kind of person you'd want to disappoint.

"Uh, Tony, you have my money, right?"

"In the trunk. Okay, which way?" the big man asked while starting the car.

"Uh, left. Just follow the signs to Waimea."

"Is there a Wal-Mart on the way?" Tony wanted to know.

"A Wal-Mart? Well, yeah. It's a couple of blocks that way, by the hospital. Why?"

"I need a few things. It won't take long."

"Hey, um, can you pick up a six-pack while you're there—for the drive?"

Tony looked at him like he was out of his mind but said, "Sure."

When they arrived at Wal-Mart, Tony parked near the back of the lot and strode into the store, taking the keys with him. Bob was getting a bad feeling about this whole deal. Maybe he should take off and offer to warn Kate for another $2,500 and be done with it. But he would be walking away from $15,000. All he had to do was point Kate out, get his money, and go. Easy. Bob tried the glove box to look for the trunk release but it was locked. Of course it was locked. There was $15,000 in cash back there. Man, he needed another beer bad. His nerves were frayed. He put his seat back and started to write a song about this whole crazy scene. He'd dozed off a bit but was jarred awake when the trunk slammed shut and Tony opened the driver's side door. Tony handed him a six-pack of cold beer but said nothing.

"Want one?" Bob asked as he twisted off the cap of his own beer.

"No. So, which way to the girl?"

"Head west," Bob said and gulped down his beer.

❋ ❋ ❋

To pass the time on the long drive across the island Bob shared what little history of the island he knew, pointing out landmarks as he saw the signs. A lot of what he said was bullshit, but this Tony guy seemed interested.

"Over there, that's an old fort, Russian I think. A lot people go there to party. There's not much left to see, but it's kinda cool to walk around in the rubble," Bob said.

"Oh yeah, is it a big tourist attraction?"

"Nah, I've been there twice and I've never seen anyone else."

"What's the soil here like," Tony asked as he waved his hand toward the cane fields on both sides of the two-lane road.

"It's red and rich. Shit seems to grow really good here," Bob said, not knowing what else to say. Then he remembered something interesting. "One of the cash crops here is pakalolo."

"Paka what?" Tony asked.

"Pot, man. You know, weed, grass… marijuana."

"I know what marijuana is. What I don't know is if the dirt is hard or soft."

"I think it's pretty soft. Why?" Tony didn't answer. "You a farmer or something?" Bob asked.

"Or something."

"What do you do?"

"I'm a writer," Tony said proudly.

"Really. That's cool, man. What do you write?" Bob said, turning in his seat to get a better look at the Tony.

"Crime novels."

"Wow, anything I may have heard of?"

"I doubt it," Tony said. "It's a very competitive field."

"Tell me about it. I had a record deal and, well, it didn't go so well. I'm a songwriter myself. That's why I need the money. I'm gonna start my own record label and then record and release my own album. That way I don't have to deal with the corporate crap."

Tony looked at him for a long moment and then turned his attention back to the road.

"What are you going to do when you find Kate? After paying me, of course," Bob said with a nervous little laugh.

"Does it really matter?"

"No. I mean… I guess not."

"All you have to do is point her out to me and I'll take it from there," Tony said.

Bob thought about it for a minute and asked, "Are you going to kill her?"

Tony smirked ever so slightly and said, "Bob, if I

told you, I'd have to kill you."

Bob laughed as if it were the funniest thing he'd ever heard. The truth was, there was nothing funny about it.

CHAPTER 27

"I can't believe you shouted my name across the room. What were you thinking?"

"Look, I said I was sorry and I am. It was a dumb thing to do. You're right, you're always right," Amy said.

"Hey, that's uncalled for."

"Okay, sorry. You're almost always right."

Kate looked across at her stepsister and realized that nothing had changed between them since the last time they'd seen one another. They just picked up right where they left off.

"You look nice," Kate said sincerely.

"Thanks. You're probably wondering where I got the money to pay for this outfit, right?"

"No. But since you mentioned it," Kate said, keeping her eyes on the road.

"I have some money of my own now, I'll have you know," Amy said, her chin up.

"I'm glad to hear it. Nice ring, by the way," Kate said, nodding at the diamond ring Amy had grabbed from the safe-deposit box.

"Do you want it back?"

"No, you can keep it."

"The necklace, too?"

"Sure, why not. They're more sentimental than valuable."

"Really? What do you think they're worth?"

"I don't know. They were gifts from my ex-boyfriend before Angel."

"Do you think they're worth over a thousand bucks?"

"Probably. Speaking of money, how much were you able to get from the agent?"

"$25,000," Amy said.

"What? That's it?" Kate snapped back.

"We were lucky to get that if you ask me," Amy said, selling it hard.

"Amy, that woman has probably made almost a million dollars off my book by now."

"Well, all she offered was $5,000 but I was able to get it up to $25,000."

"Fine. Where is the money?"

Amy pulled out a big fat envelope—which was a lot fatter before she kept taking a bigger and bigger cut for herself. She handed the cash to Kate as she drove. Kate took it, tempted to pull over and count it, but she knew that would be rude. She'd count it later.

"Thanks," Kate said as she slipped the envelope into her bag.

Amy didn't say anything when she passed the envelope over to Kate but glanced in the rearview mirror and noticed the same cab behind them that had been following them since they left the airport. It could be a coincidence, but she didn't think so. Still, she didn't think she should say anything.

Kate looked at Amy and said, "What?"

"What do you mean, what?" Amy replied.

"I said 'thanks' and you didn't say anything," Kate noted.

"Oh, sorry. I was looking at something. You're welcome. So you think the agent will make a million bucks off your book. How much of that would have been yours if you weren't, well, dead?" Amy asked.

"I don't know, about $850,000, give or take."

"Are you kidding me? $850,000 dollars! Why don't you just go back and get it?" Amy demanded.

"It's complicated. For one, Angel would kill me, for sure. For another, it's not about the money. I like my life the way it is. For the first time in a long time, I'm happy. Look around. It's beautiful here, don't you think?" Kate said as they turned off Kaumuali' Highway 50 toward onto Maluhia Road on the way to Poipu and went through the famous tree tunnel. Amy looked back and the cab took the same turnoff.

"Couldn't you just go back, get the money, and hire some really good body guards to protect you? You'd be famous."

"You're not listening. I'm not going back."

"So what did you need the money for?"

"I need to move to another island and start all over again."

"Which island?"

"Maui," Kate said, passing a pineapple truck.

"When?" Amy asked.

"I have a few things to take of first."

"Like what?"

"First, I'm going to buy a sailboat and then sail over."

"Why don't you just fly?"

"With a sailboat I'll have a place to stay when I get there."

"You're gonna live on a boat? You?" Amy said.

"I've changed. I don't need to have all the trappings I used to have. I want to live a simple life."

"Are you going to at least get a big boat?"

At the three-way stop in Old Koloa, Kate glared at Amy. "I had planned on getting a bigger boat, but since we were only able to get $25,000 from the agent, I guess I'll be looking for boats in the $15,000 to $20,000 range. For that kind of money, I don't know what I can get. We'll see."

"I already said $25,000 was the most I could get."

"I know. I know. It's alright. Don't worry about it. I told you, money isn't as important to me as it used to be."

"Can I come with you to Maui?"

"Don't you have to get back to your daughter and your job?"

"Well, yeah. How long will it take to sail to Maui?"

"The way I want to do it, a few days so we can do a little sightseeing on the way."

"I want to go."

"You're sure?"

"Yeah, count me in."

"Okay."

"Is this where you live?" Amy asked as they pulled into The Sands.

"It's only temporary."

CHAPTER 28

"I found her," Manuel announced through the phone.

Angel slammed his hand against the wall of his cell. "I knew it. Fucking bitch."

"Yeah."

"How did you find her?"

"It was part luck and part persistence. It wasn't easy; she's a tricky one. It's a good thing she got careless or comfortable, but I found her," Manuel said.

"Did you take care of our problem?"

"Not yet. I bought a camera with a long lens and I have some great shots of her. There is no doubt it's Kate and she's not dead. These pictures prove beyond a reasonable doubt that she's alive and well in Hawaii."

"Manny, you don't understand, I don't want her to be found alive. I need her dead. The sooner the better."

"Fine."

"One more thing: make it look like an accident—a fall from a cliff, a drowning, something like that. Manny, I wish I could be there with you, bro."

"Me, too. Me, too. We, uh, do have a problem, though."

"What."

"There's someone with her," Manuel said.

"A man!"

"No, a woman. Good looking. She came in from the mainland."

"Do them both," Angel said as if he were ordering a pizza.

"That's gonna cost extra, Angel."

"Jesus, Manny. We go way back. Can't you just do it as a favor?"

"No. This place ain't cheap. I'm wracking up some serious expenses here—which I'm not charging you for. A double homicide, that's twice the risk so it's gonna be twice the price. You can afford it, Angel." There was a long pause. "Angel?"

"Alright. But make sure it looks like an accident. We don't want this coming back to bite us."

"Agreed. It's not like I need that either. I'll call you next week at the usual time," Manuel said, satisfied he was going to get what the job was worth. He had a reputation to uphold. He couldn't go around offing for people free. That kind of stuff had a way of getting around.

※ ※ ※

Angel closed the phone and turned it off. He didn't have a charger for the contraband device so he had to be careful about preserving the battery. He hid it and lied back on his bunk and stared at the ceiling. Soon this would be over and he could get the hell out of here and back to doing what he loved more than anything—banging girls he met across the country… and playing baseball. He wasn't worried about his image. He would play up

the bad boy image if he had to. Or, when he was exoner-
ated he could get a lot of mileage out of being the victim.
Either way, he would bounce back. He started thinking
about all the ways he could spend Kate's money before
drifting off to sleep.

CHAPTER 29

"Look, she was here when I called you guys. I swear to you," Bob pleaded.

Tony just stared at him. "You said she was staying here. You said she worked here. Neither of those statements were accurate, were they? She don't live here and she don't work here no more. This is not good, Bob."

"Let me think. Let me think. There's got to be a way to find her. It's not a big island. She always carried around this silver Apple laptop computer. Maybe if we bought one just like it and left it at the front desk saying we found it, they would call her and she would come to get it. We could wait until she comes back."

"Bob, if she ain't missing her computer, why would she come back to get it?"

"Uh, how about this? We could tap the phones to see where the front desk calls to contact her," Bob said, desperate now.

"Tap the phones. You know how to do that?" Tony asked.

"No, but I thought maybe you did."

"Even if I did, where do you plan to get a laptop to leave behind?"

"We buy one. We can use the money from the

trunk," Bob was getting excited as his plan started to come together.

Tony thought about it. It might work. They wouldn't have to tap the phones, they just had to distract the woman at the front desk long enough to look at the caller ID after she called Kate. There was probably a reverse directory at the library with the address.

"Okay, we'll try it your way. You know exactly what kind of computer she had, right?"

"Oh, yeah. I know for a fact it was a brand-new Apple PowerBook because I've had my eye on one for my new recording studio," Bob said. "We can buy one at the Kukui Grove Shopping Center. It's not that far from here."

"Okay, but we do this my way. You do exactly what I tell you. You got that?"

"Yeah, yeah, sure. Whatever you say, 'T'."

"Did you just call me 'T'?" Tony asked.

Bob shrugged and said, "Yeah."

"Don't" was Tony's reply as he walked away.

✳ ✳ ✳

After Tony bought the laptop with his stolen credit card, the two drove back to the west side of the island, discussing the plan along the way. Tony parked behind the West Side Brewing Company and walked back around to the bar where he ordered a diet soda and a sandwich. Bob came back from delivering the laptop to the front desk, sat at the other end of the bar and gave Tony the signal that everything was going as planned. There was only one person working, Vina, the clerk Bob knew Kate was friendly with. Vina recognized the laptop as Kate's, but didn't quite buy the story that Bob had just found it in the bar like he'd said. She figured he'd stolen it from her and now wanted to return it out of guilt or for a reward. Either way, she should probably call Kate and find out what was going on. Tony asked the bartender where the front desk was and made his way there, saying he'd be right back. On his way to the lobby he stopped at the bathroom and using a towel patted water on his forehead and the front of his XXXL shirt. Once inside the lobby he looked around at the photos and then went to the front desk making a production of patting his forehead with a wet paper towel. "I was wondering," Tony said as he put his hand on the counter to brace himself, "if you had any rooms available."

"Yes, we do. Sir, are you okay? You don't look so good," Vina said, clearly concerned.

Tony bent forward but raised his hand as if to say, I'm okay.

"Are you sure?" Vina asked.

Tony collapsed on the floor in a big heap.

"Oh my God. Oh my God!" Vina yelled as she came around the counter to check on Tony who was now face down on the floor, not moving. Vina tried to turn him over and Tony gave an Oscar-worthy performance, making himself as heavy as possible; then he allowed his eyes to roll back in his head as she finally pushed him over. Vina checked to see if he was breathing. Just then he opened his eyes and said, "What happened? Why am I on the floor?"

"Oh my God. You, you passed out and fell. I thought you were, uh… I'm just glad you're not, um… Are you okay?"

Vina struggled to push Tony into a sitting position. "I feel a little lightheaded, but I'm okay," he said.

Tony was in terrible shape and overweight. He could have easily been a victim of a heart attack, stroke, or diabetic seizure. "I should call 9-1-1," Vina said.

"No, no, no. Can you help me to the bathroom? I just need to splash some water on my face and get something to drink and I'll be fine."

"I don't know, sir. You really looked like you were out of it there. I mean, maybe I should call a doctor."

"Trust me, I'll be fine. I just need some water and then get some food in me. If you'll just help me to the bathroom and if you don't mind, get me a glass of water, I'd really appreciate it."

"Of course."

Vina helped Tony to his feet and to the restroom before going to the bar to get a glass of water, leaving the front desk unattended. Bob slipped in the other door and checked the caller ID. Someone had just used the phone to make a local call. The other calls stored in the phone were all made before he left the laptop. Bingo. Bob wrote the number down and went back to the bar to see Vina helping Tony back onto his bar stool.

"Dan, make sure he eats this sandwich and drinks a lot of water and keep an eye on him," Vina said to the bartender. "Sir, did you want to reserve a room for the night? It might be a good idea."

"I'll be fine. Don't worry. I'm gonna go to that hospital you recommended as soon as I'm feeling up to it. Thanks for everything. I really appreciate it."

"It's nothing," she said with a smile. "I have to get back to the front desk."

"Go, go," Tony said, waving her on.

※ ※ ※

Tony wolfed down his sandwich, paid his bill, and went to the Caddy where Bob was waiting for him holding the laptop. "Did you get the number?"

Bob smiled, "Yup."

"Give it to me."

"Here. What about the laptop?" Bob asked as he held the Apple PowerBook.

Tony took the slip of paper and put it in his shirt pocket. "You can keep it. Now get in."

"Thanks, man. Where we going?"

"Show me where that Russian Fort is. I'd like to see that for myself."

"But it's getting dark. What about the phone number?"

"That will have to wait until tomorrow. I need to get to a library to look it up in the reverse directory."

"Can we at least stop for some beers on the way?" Bob begged.

"Sure."

Tony pulled over at a small market in the middle of the town of Waimea so Bob could run in and grab some beer. While he waited he pulled the piece of paper out of his pocket and called information to see if he could find out where the number would lead. He was told it was the front desk of The Sands, a condo complex in a place on the south side of the island called Poipu. All he needed to know now is what Kate looked like and he could proceed with his plan. Bob got back in the car and had already polished off a beer just walking from the store to the door.

"Thanks. I needed that," he said as he cracked another one.

"I need you to tell me what Kate looks like," Tony paused and added, "So I can stake out wherever she's staying."

"When do I get my money?"

"When we get to the Russian Fort, I'll give you your money."

"You have it all—$15,000? That's what the agent promised."

"Yeah, I got your 15 K. That was a good idea you had about the laptop."

"Thanks. Maybe I could get a bonus for finding her twice," Bob said in all seriousness.

"*Fottere*!" Tony yelled, "You got some balls, you know that?"

"Thanks. I'm guessing 'fottere' doesn't mean we're friends in Italian, eh, Tony?"

Tony just rolled his eyes. "About Kate's description…"

Bob let out a long breath of air and began. "She's about 5-foot-4 and has bleached-blond hair, cut short. She's got a great body. Big boobs. I'd guess they're fake, but I can't say for sure. Um, she wears a lot of hats. Oh, and she drives a red Jeep."

Tony started the car and headed back to the other side of the island as the sun set behind them.

"Turn here," Bob said as he pointed to a sign that read, *Fort Elizabeth State Historical Park*. A dirt road led the way. "You should see this place during the day. Great view."

There was nobody there when Tony parked the car in the dirt lot and said, "Drink up."

"Want the last one?" Bob asked, his hand anticipating Tony's negative reply.

"Nope. You go ahead. Then we'll go get your money out of the trunk."

Bob guzzled the beer, then the two guys got out into the twilight. Tony used his key to open the trunk and said as he handed Bob a rather heavy briefcase, "I bet you'll want to count the money, huh."

"Nah, I trust you guys."

"Count it anyway. That way there won't be a problem in the future."

"Okay, if you insist," Bob said as he set the case down on the ground. He was giddy now. "Wow, this is heavy. I guess that's what $15,000 feels like." Bob fiddled with the latches and said, "Hey, Tony, the case is locked."

"I know," Tony said as he swung a shovel, striking Bob on the side of the head. The sound of metal on bone cut through the warm twilight air as Tony hit him again and again until he was sure Bob was dead. It was likely the first blow killed him, but Tony was sick of listening to the little weasel talk and gave a couple of extra swings out of pent-up frustration. Tony bent down to check for breathing and quickly noticed that Bob's brains were leaking onto the dirt. "Shit!"

The plan was to drag the body off the beaten path and bury it deep enough so it wouldn't be found for weeks—if ever. Now Tony would have to clean up a little before he moved the body to its final resting place. This was not the first person Tony had killed. In fact, as best he could recall, this was number eleven. Kate would make it an even dozen. Maybe he could finally get out of this line of work and concentrate on his writing. His criminal mind is what made him such a good writer. He had lived the life. He knew what it was like to kill. He knew how to avoid getting caught, too. By hitting Bob from behind, he made sure the splatter pattern of blood and brains wouldn't be on his clothes or the car.

※ ※ ※

In addition to the shovel, Tony had also bought other gardening supplies at Wal-Mart, including a cooler, gloves, overalls, boots, a saw, an ax, pruning shears, burlap sacks, and fertilizer. He'd contemplated buying gasoline and burning the body, but the fire might attract attention. Burying it in several different spots seemed like the way to go. It was going to be a long night, so Tony began the process—one piece at a time, but for Bob's severed right hand, which he put in a cooler. With that, he could plant evidence—fingerprints, DNA, and blood—at the crime scene where Kate Ramirez would be found murdered by Bob Sommers.

CHAPTER 30

Mary had planned on staying in one of the lesser expensive hotels in Kapaa, but now she found herself at the front desk of The Sands in Poipu trying to get a room near Kate's.

"I don't want a room overlooking the ocean, I want one with a garden view," Mary insisted.

"But for the same price you can look out at the waves breaking right there in front of your lanai."

"My what?"

"Your patio."

After following the Jeep from the airport, Mary knew what room Kate was in and her goal was to get as close as possible. Kate was staying in a second-floor garden-view room in building 5, overlooking a large lawn and the pool. Mary hoped to be located above, below, or beside that room.

"How about this room?" Mary asked as she pointed to the room next to Kate's on the map.

"Let me check. Mmmmm, I'm sorry, it's booked."

So were the other rooms around Kate's. Mary had an idea. She looked at the map again and chose a room on the second floor in building 3, on the other side of the lawn and across from the pool—facing Kate's room.

"That room is right next to the ice machine and the elevator. You sure you want it?"

"Yes."

"Do you need help with your bags?" the front desk clerk asked, looking at the small carry-on Mary was toting behind her.

"Actually, I left the rest of my luggage at baggage claim and I don't have a rental car. Do you know how I can have it delivered here?"

"What airline?"

"United."

"I'll take care of it. My uncle works for United. I'll have him drop your bag off on his way home. It's no problem."

"Really? Wow, thanks," Mary said as she grabbed her key. This wasn't a problem. The truth was, the room Mary had chosen hadn't been booked in months. Nobody wanted it because of the location and the noise. The owners who put it in the rental pool were constantly complaining about the lack of revenue. If Mary were to have an extended stay in this unit, then it was worth a little extra effort. "Oh, by the way, you don't happen to know anyone in the rental-car business, by chance?"

"My Auntie works for Alamo, but we have a Budget office here on property. The desk is right over there," she said pointing at one of the two empty desks across the lobby. "Go ahead and walk over there and I'll find someone to take care of you."

Mary couldn't believe her good fortune. Not only did she find Kate within minutes of stepping off the plane, she also found the nicest, most helpful person on the island to assist her.

"I'll be right back. Can I leave my bag here?" Mary asked.

"Sure, Kalani will be here in a few minutes to help you with your rental car," the nice lady said as she put her hand over the receiver on the phone.

Mary wanted to be sure that Kate hadn't left her room. She went outside the lobby where, looking up, she saw the drapes were closed but the lights were on.

"Good work, Mary," she said out loud, but to no one in particular, "Now what?"

Mary thought she saw someone peeking through the curtains, but she wasn't sure. "Don't stand there staring at the window like an idiot," Mary cursed herself as she headed back to the lobby to get a car, passing a big man in a red aloha shirt smoking a cigar.

CHAPTER 31

"What are you looking at?" Kate asked Amy who was peering out the window.

"Nothing. I just wanted to see what the view was like. Why didn't you get a room overlooking the ocean?" Amy said, closing the blinds again.

"I was lucky to get this room. Besides, I'm not on vacation, and neither are you. You're here to help me," Kate said while she made tea for them.

"How about that."

"How about what?" Kate asked.

"Me helping you. It used to be the other way around. My how times have changed. Kate The Great needs my help."

"That's right. I have helped you out of a lot of jams and now I need you to be there for me."

Amy looked out the window again. The woman was gone but the big fat man was still down there smoking his cigar and trying to look like he wasn't staring at their room.

"You're right. There was a time when we were close. Then you turned your back on me," Amy stated bitterly.

"I said I was sorry and as soon as all this is over I

will make it up to you. Here, I made you some tea."

"Make it up to me how?" Amy asked, taking the tea.

"I don't know. Maybe when I get settled on Maui you and your daughter can come stay with me."

"You don't even know her name, do you?" Amy asked incredulously.

"Sure I do. It's Jenna."

"It's Jenny. Jenny! Jeez, Kate."

"I was close."

"Close doesn't cut it, Kate. You should know your own niece's name."

"Step-niece."

"Oh, right. She's not your real niece and I'm not your real sister. You know what, I'm outta here."

"What do you mean you're out of here? Amy!"

"I mean, I need to get some air." And with that, Amy left the room, slamming the door on her way out.

"Fine. Go," Kate said. She actually knew her step-niece's name, but she wanted to start a fight with Amy so she would storm off and leave her stuff behind. It worked. Kate looked out the window and watched Amy walk across the lawn before going through her luggage. Sure enough, there was an envelope with what looked to be almost $20,000 in it. Kate knew her sister well enough to expect she would skim some money from the agent, but $20,000? Amy was more of a bitch than she remembered.

❄ ❄ ❄

Amy's plan to get into an argument with her sister

also worked like a charm; she needed to get out of the room without arousing any suspicion. On her way out the door, she grabbed the manuscript Kate had tried to hide under a bunch of nautical charts and sailing books on the kitchen counter. Amy wanted to know what Kate had planned. She would skim the pages and put them back in place before Kate even knew they were missing. But first there was someone she wanted to talk to.

CHAPTER 32

"Ms. Golding, Erin White from the Lifetime Network is on line 1," Carol announced to her boss over the intercom.

"No word from Paramount?" Sandi shot back.

"I've left three messages for Mr. Marshall, but his office hasn't responded," Carol replied, realizing early on what a long shot it was, but she made the calls anyway.

"Fine, put her through," Sandi barked back.

"Hi Erin, how can I help you?" Sandi said as nice as could be.

"I hear you're shopping the rights to *Angel* around," the Lifetime executive stated.

"That's true. It's with Paramount and Universal right now."

"I read the book, and I think it would be a perfect fit for us."

Sandi knew that a meant a made-for-TV movie, not the big blockbuster she hoped for. "I really see this book being optioned as a feature film."

"I see. Well, if you change your mind, we're ready to make an offer and we have the lead lined up."

"Really? Who?" Sandi asked too quickly to hide her true desire to sell the rights to whomever would pay her price.

"Teri Hatcher. She read the book and loved it. She's convinced she's the perfect pick to play the wife."

"Teri Hatcher. Hmmmm. What's your offer?"

"We are willing to go as high as $1 million," the TV executive said, as if that amount of money meant nothing.

"Erin, I've got to be honest, that's not going to be enough," Sandi said, her standard answer to initial offers. She's been playing this game for a long time.

"What are you looking for?"

"$5 million," Sandi blurted out with no basis for that price. It just sounded like a good counterproposal to $1 million.

"Whew. That's not in the budget for this project. Keep in mind a movie like this would boost book sales. Think about the benefits of having this project green-lighted right into production with a name star attached. Get back to me if you can work within our budget. I'd really like to see this book be made into a movie."

"So would I. So would I," Sandi said, knowing she should be able to get over a million dollars for the rights.

"I'll talk to you next week then. We want to get this into production and out while the story is hot, you understand."

"Of course. I'll get back to you as soon as I have an answer for you."

"Okay, but it's my understanding that you hold all the rights to the book. Correct?"

"Yes, that is correct."

"I hope we can work together on this, Sandi. We

plan to shoot on location in Hawaii. You could come on set if you'd like," the television executive said, upping the ante.

"Hawaii, huh? That sounds great, Erin. I'll talk to my team and get back to you soon. Thanks again for the interest in the book and the offer."

Sandi quickly found her inner bitch again and pushed the intercom button. "Carol! Get me Mr. Marshall at Paramount. We need to light a fire under his ass."

"I'll try, but he isn't taking your calls."

"Well, maybe you're not leaving the right messages. Try again and make it sound urgent."

Carol rolled her eyes and said, "I'll get right on it, Ms. Golding."

Sandi leaned back in her office chair and gazed out at the New York skyline. Hawaii looked pretty good from here. Besides, with all the money going out to hit men and blackmailers, Sandi was feeling the pinch. Sure, she stood to clear several hundred thousand dollars with the Lifetime deal, but she'd hoped the movie deal would put her over the top and into the millions of dollars. Maybe she should just take Erin's offer and be done with it. Surely they would go to at least $1.5 million without much pushing. Optioning the book to Paramount would mean more money, but the picture could take years to get made—if it ever did. No, if she could get Erin closer to $2 million, she would make the deal.

"Carol, get Erin from Lifetime on the phone," Sandi ordered.

"I have Mr. Gravano is holding on line 2, Ms. Golding," Carol replied back.

"Put him through."

"Hello, Tony. How's the writing going?"

"I, uh, huh?" the low-level mobster wasn't grasping the meaning of what Sandi was really asking.

"Did you write the ending we talked about?" Sandi said, trying to get Tony to understand what 'ending' meant.

"Oh, uh, one chapter down, one to go."

"Which chapter did you finish first?"

"The, uh, the one with the singer. I'm working on the ending to the chapter with the writer in it."

"How far along are you?"

"I know how it's gonna end; I just need to find a place to write it. I should have it done in a day or so."

"Good. I can't wait to read it when you're finished."

"I'm real close to wrapping it up. I'll let you know when I'm done with the 'book'."

Sandi hung up the phone. Hmmm. Maybe Tony wasn't the imbecile she thought he was. Maybe she actually could get a book of his published. He certainly knew what he was talking about when it came to murder.

CHAPTER 33

Kate finished packing and was able to fit her entire life into one large suitcase. In the old days she'd need two suitcases just to go to Palm Springs for the weekend. Amy had packed light, too. Kate noticed that a lot of Amy's clothes still had the price tags on them. She was obviously living large off her money. Kate wasn't going to make a federal case about it… now. It was early in the morning and Kate wanted to get down to Hanalei Bay, where her new boat was waiting. When she and Angel bought the Sea Ray, the amount of paperwork and the time it took to complete the transaction was staggering. This time she wasn't buying the boat from a broker, but rather from one half of a couple who had sailed over from California. The trip had proved too much for their relationship and they split up. He hooked up with a waitress and planned on staying. She was flying back to the mainland—heartbroken, but she would get even with the schmuck by selling the boat. The title was in her name and she wanted to get rid of it and get on with her life. The 33-foot Hunter sailboat was worth a lot more than Kate had to offer, but she hoped she had enough to use as a down payment and she would pay off the balance a little at a time. Kate first met the boat's owner when the woman was sitting on a bench in the courtyard of The Sands crying—and staring up at Kate's room for hours on end. Against her better judgment, Kate decided to talk to her to find out what the hell was going on. It turned out her boyfriend and the waitress he was screwing were living in the condo above Kate's. Having been cooped up on a boat with this creep for two months and then dumped by "the love of her life," this poor girl needed someone to talk to and a shoulder to cry on. When it came to being cheated on, Kate was an expert and was able to talk the distraught girl off the ledge. After hours of discussion, some of them on the sailboat, Kate had convinced her the previous day to go back to the mainland and start over. To make it easier, Kate would buy the boat for cash—or at least make a cash down-payment. If Amy hadn't embezzled over $20,000 from her, she could have almost bought the boat outright. The sloop was perfect for her plans. The design made it easy to sail, but was fairly fast. The wide beam of the boat created a very roomy interior with a massive salon, large stateroom, and a full galley.

"So where is this boat you're buying?" Amy asked.

"It's on the other side of the island."

"When are we leaving?"

"In a few minutes," Kate said, doing her last-minute check of the condo, including wiping the place down to remove any trace she was ever there.

"Do you mind if I go to the lobby store before we leave so I can pick up a few items?"

"Amy, we're stopping at the market to get provisions for the trip. You can get whatever you need there."

"Fine. I want to call Jenny before we go, then."

"So call."

"I'd like to do it in private if you don't mind."

"You want me to leave?"

"I can go outside and call."

Just then the condo's phone rang and Amy picked it up. "Hello." Kate shot her a dirty look. There was no reason to answer the phone. Nobody knew she was there.

"It's for you. Gina something," Amy said.

"Vina?" Kate corrected her.

Amy shrugged, handed her the phone, then stepped outside.

"Hello?"

"It's me, Vina. Who answered the phone?"

"Oh, that was my sister."

"I didn't know you had a sister," Vina said.

"Stepsister."

"Hey, remember when I called you about the laptop? It got me thinking, that was a really strange coincidence. I don't know what Bob was after, but maybe he wanted me to call you for no-good reasons. I just thought of that, and I am sorry if I screwed up."

"You didn't. It was totally possible Bob could have taken my laptop, the little creep. You did the right thing to call. Where's the laptop now?"

"That's the strange thing, it's gone."

"That is odd. It's not worth worrying about. I paid Bob to keep his mouth shut, I don't see why he'd come looking for me."

"Maybe he wants more money for his silence?"

"Hmm. That's possible."

"Have you seen Bob lurking around the bushes at The Sands?" Vina asked.

"No, I can't say that I have."

"How about a big, hairy Italian guy?"

That made Kate pause. Didn't she see a guy fitting that description last night? Yes, there was a big man across the lawn smoking a cigar just last night. Could Bob be here, too?

"Vina, thank you for the warning. I'm leaving the island today and I want you to have my Jeep. It's totally paid for and I signed the pink slip over to you and left it under the seat."

"What? Where are you going?"

"It might be better if I don't say. I'll leave the Jeep at the dinghy landing in Hanalei, right by the lifeguard tower, or I could leave it by the pier if that's easier."

"I can't just take your Jeep. Let me pay you something for it."

"Vina, I want you to have it. I owe you and this is my way of repaying you."

"Kate, I'm worried about you. Why are you leaving the Jeep on the opposite side of the island? Just tell me where you're going so if something happens, at least someone will know where you are."

"I guess that makes sense. I bought a sailboat and it's anchored in Hanalei Bay. Amy and I are gonna set sail for Oahu first thing in the morning and then cruise to Maui. My stepsister has a cell phone so I'll call you along the way if I can. Otherwise, I'll call you from Maui next week when I get settled."

"What about your stepsister?"

"In the beginning I need a little help sailing the boat, but once I'm there I'm going to send her packing. I may even drop her off on Oahu—or Ni' ihau."

"Ni' ihau, right. That's funny. It's because of people like your sister that the island is off limits to outsiders. Be careful Kate, and call me when you can."

"I will, Vina, and thanks for everything. You're a true friend."

"Mahalo for the Jeep. I really needed my own car, so this is perfect."

"It's the least I can do for you, Vina."

"Kate, before you go, what kind of boat did you buy and what's the name?"

"It's a 33-foot sailboat with blue accents. You'll love this. Painted on the transom is the name the previous owners picked: *The Great Escape*."

"Perfect."

CHAPTER 34

"Amy, look behind us but don't be too obvious," Kate said without turning her head.

"What am I looking for?"

"See that silver car? It's been following us since we left the parking lot," Kate said, pointing up at the rear-view mirror. "I'm pulling into the shopping center on the left. Let's see if he follows us." She turned into the Rainbow Shopping Center in Kapaa, and the Caddy kept going; the driver, however, craned his neck to look back as he drove by. "Did you see that?" Kate said in a hushed voice. "He looked right at me when he went by."

"You're just paranoid. He looked like a tourist to me. Maybe he was checking us out and wants to hook up." That Amy would even come up with this possibility was completely opposite of Kate's thinking.

"I don't know. He looked like a guy Vina thinks was looking for me at the place I was staying in before."

"Well, he's gone now."

"I guess so. I think I'm gonna double back before we head to Hanalei just to be on the safe side."

"What?" Amy asked.

"Why take any chances?"

"You're losing it, Kate. You've been on the run way too long."

"And you haven't been on the run long enough to know what it's like." Kate paused in thought for a moment. "I don't know, maybe you're right. Come on, let's go shopping. We need to get enough stuff to last at least a week and this is as good a place as any to stock up. Hey, do you still drink Yoo-hoos?" Kate asked, trying to ease the tension between them.

Amy wasn't paying attention. She was looking around to see if the silver car had come back into the center. "What?"

"I asked if you still drink Yoo-hoos?"

"Oh. Uh, no. That was, like, years ago."

"Well, I made a list of the things we need. Just grab anything else you want to eat or drink. Okay?"

"Yeah, sure," Amy said as she glanced back one last time before they went into the grocery store.

※ ※ ※

"The problem with this Jeep is there's no storage," Kate said a short time later, cramming the coolers filled with groceries into any nook and cranny that wasn't occupied by their luggage. Amy just watched. Kate made it fit, but there wasn't an inch to spare. "Thanks for all your help," she said sarcastically. "On the boat, you're going to have to do a lot more than that, you know."

"Fine."

"What's wrong with you?" Kate asked.

"Nothing. I'm… I guess I'm a little nervous about

the trip. I don't have any experience on a boat. What if I get seasick?"

Kate reached back into one of the grocery bags and pulled out a box of Dramamine. "You can take these."

Kate looked around before backing the Jeep out and said, "Looks like you were right. The silver car's gone. Good."

The silver car was gone—because Tony was now driving a stolen black Dodge Durango. It took less than five minutes to find another car in the parking lot, break the window, and hotwire it. This also gave him time to study a map of the island. Tony pulled out onto the roadway one car back from the Jeep—just to be sure he wasn't recognized, which wouldn't be hard to do, thanks to the stop-and-go traffic in the tiny town of Kapaa. Tony was surprised so many people passed through this way.

A short while later, it became harder for Tony to remain inconspicuous as they got out onto the open road. From the map, he had picked the perfect place to run the Jeep off the road at a spot coming up soon. As they rounded the long curve that led to the north side of the island, Tony passed the minivan that was between him and Kate's Jeep. Now all he had to do was wait. Kate noticed the black SUV behind her but didn't give it a second thought. Her mind was occupied with all the things that needed to be done before they set sail. All of a sudden, the SUV was alongside her. Tony put the passenger window down and was signaling for her to pull over. She recognized him as the same big guy in the silver Cadillac.

"Kate, pull over!" Amy screamed.

"No!"

"He's got a gun!"

"I didn't see a gun," Kate said as she pressed the accelerator to get away. The SUV immediately rammed the Jeep, sending it skittering off the road and onto the grass. "Shit!" Kate screamed as she fought the wheel, trying to gain control of the car. The SUV swung over again but Kate avoided the charge.

"Jesus, Kate, please pull over! I don't want to die." Amy gripped the door tightly.

"Hang on."

Kate swung the wheel to the right, and the Jeep bounced down a dirt road she had discovered several weeks ago while searching for a hiking trail. They were going way too fast for the terrain but they were putting distance between themselves and the black SUV.

"When we get to the bottom of this road, I want you to jump out as fast as you can and follow me. Got it?" Amy nodded and undid her seatbelt to be ready to go when they stopped. "Did you hear me?"

"I'll be right behind you," Amy affirmed with another nod.

"Ready?"

Kate slammed the brakes just in front of a gate at the end of the dirt road. Beyond the gate was a short path through the trees leading to a deserted beach. The Jeep kicked up a cloud of red dust as the two of them jumped out of the Jeep and ran for the sand.

"Come on. Hurry. We've got to cross that river over there and get around those rocks before that guy gets here. Run, Amy, run!"

Kate was either in much better shape than her stepsister or she was more motivated. She got to the stream first and had to wait a few seconds for a very out-of-breath Amy to get there. Kate grabbed her hand and pulled her into the knee-deep water that was running a good three knots, feeding into the ocean. This made the crossing take longer than the 20 yards should have.

When they were across, Kate looked back to see the big guy lumbering down the beach as fast as a guy his size could. They had a head start, but they needed to get up and around the point so that they could make their move. Kate knew the area because she had come here to check out the blowhole around the bend. She was less sure about what was on the other side of the point. Amy was clearly struggling, but every second counted, so Kate screamed at her.

"Come on, Amy. Run, dammit!" The lava rock they were traversing was wet and slippery, not to mention uneven and sharp.

"I'm doing the best I can. Go on without me, I'll catch up," Amy said between breaths.

"I'm not leaving you behind!"

A minute later, they made it around the point and past the blowhole, only to discover that the rest of the way was impassable.

"This is your plan?" Amy asked. "To get us cornered in a place with the ocean on one side and a steep cliff on the other—with nobody around to help us?"

Kate looked up. "We've got to climb, then. It's the only way out. It may even lead back to the car."

"Kate, are you crazy? Look at that cliff. It's almost straight up."

"We can do it. Come on Amy, let's go."

"You don't even know what this guy wants. Maybe he…"

"Maybe he what?" Kate got right in Amy's face and yelled, "He followed us from the hotel and then he tried to run us off the road. That's all I need to know."

Kate didn't wait for a response. Instead, she turned back around and started climbing the cliff. Fortunately, there were solid hand- and foot-holds, and she was able to quickly work her way up. Amy was going a lot slower. From her vantage point, Kate was able to see the big guy making his way across the lava rocks. He wasn't moving fast, but he was getting closer and Amy was taking her sweet time. It was as if she were afraid to break a nail or scuff her shoes. If she could catch up, they could be up and over the top before he even knew where they were. Instead, he was going to know exactly where they went. Damn her. Kate went ahead and climbed up and over the top. From there she could see the Jeep in the distance and a trail leading there. If Amy could just move her ass, they could make it to the Jeep well before the big guy could climb the cliff or work his way back along the rocks and up the beach. Kate looked back over the edge of the cliff. It didn't even seem like Amy had moved.

"Come on! You can rest when you get up here."

"I'm scared of heights."

"No, you're not. Move it!" Kate saw the big guy round the corner and look up. "Amy, if you don't get your ass up here right now I'm leaving you behind. I swear." That seemed to motivate her to move a little quicker. Meanwhile, the big guy was cursing and pointing at them. "What is your problem?" Kate yelled down at him.

"You're dead! I swear to God, I'm going to kill you both," Tony yelled as he started his way up the cliff, surprisingly fast for a guy in his shape and size. Amy finally made it to the top and Kate pulled her up and over the edge.

"Leave us alone!" Kate screamed at him.

"I can't do that," he yelled up from a perch about twenty-five feet up the 100-foot cliff.

"Can't we talk about this," Amy yelled back down, "and work something out?"

Kate shot her a dirty look.

"That's a good idea," Tony replied. "Just stay right there, I'll be right up. Deal?" Kate replied by grabbing one of the loose lava rocks and tossing it down at him. Tony ducked as it sailed over his head. "Are you crazy? What did you do that for?" Tony was now still, hesitant to continue up the cliff.

"That was my answer. You want me to make it clearer?" Kate threw another rock down, this one missing wide right.

"Okay, okay." Tony put a hand up in surrender. "I'll just meet you at your new boat instead. Fuck this shit." He made a motion with his hand like he was tipping his cap and said, "Ladies."

With that, Kate lost all restraint and started hurling rock after rock at him in fury. The first one hit him in the shoulder. The next one hit him on his back as he tried to retreat back down the cliff. When Tony looked up and saw several rocks coming his way, he instinctively covered his head, causing him lose his balance. Kate watched as he fell at least 20 feet and landed on his head. He was motionless.

"Oh my God, you killed him!" Amy said, putting her hands to her mouth and repeating over and over, "You killed him."

Kate shook her head and said, "No I didn't. He fell. You saw it. The rocks didn't even hit him."

"I know what I saw, Kate. That guy is dead. Oh my God."

Tony remained at the bottom of the cliff, his arms and legs in unnatural positions. The two stared at the body for a full minute, but there was no movement.

Kate's hands started shaking as her adrenaline rush subsided; she couldn't catch her breath. She had killed a man. Killed him. Had her desire to live a quiet life away from her psychopathic husband led to a man's death? She would have to report this to the police. A man was dead. Her dream of escaping to another island was over.

Amy took charge of the situation. "Come on, Kate. Get it together. Let's get out of here. Now!"

"We can't just leave him there."

"Why not?" Amy countered.

"We have to file a police report and explain what happened."

"Don't be ridiculous! What we need to do is stick to the plan and get the hell out of here."

Kate had a sudden look of realization on her face. "Didn't he say he'd meet us at the boat? How did he know where we were going?"

"I don't know," Amy said, tugging at Kate's arm. "But it doesn't matter because he's dead."

"He could have told someone."

"Then we'll be careful."

They both took one last look at the dead man. "He fell, right?" Kate asked, hoping for further confirmation that she was no killer.

"Yeah, Kate," Amy replied, mustering up a consoling tone. "He fell."

A short time later, Kate and Amy arrived at the Jeep. The black SUV was parked right behind them, blocking them in.

"Give me the keys," Amy said. "I can get us out of this."

Kate handed her the keys to the Jeep. Amy fired up the engine and began working the vehicle back and forth with small turns, trying to get around the Durango. At the same time, Kate walked up to the SUV and, using her shirt, opened the door handle and climbed in, wiping her fingerprints as she went. She wasn't sure what she would find, but it quickly became clear this car was stolen. The papers in the glove box indicated it belonged to a local. The guy chasing after them was anything but local. Fortunately, Kate didn't open the cooler in the back seat, or she would've found Bob's severed hand. Instead, the SUV was a dead end—literally.

CHAPTER 35

It didn't take long for Mary to find the area courthouse in downtown Lihue. She had a nose for these things. The police station was conveniently located right next to it and, curiously, so was an elementary school, a library, and a park. Feeling she would have better rapport with her counterpart on the island, rather than the police, Mary made her way to the local prosecutor's office. After explaining the situation to a very competent and cordial attorney, Mary was led over to meet the Chief of Police. Mary quickly filled him in on Angel, Kate, and what she had found so far since arriving on the island.

"I wish you had come to me first," the Chief of Police said, "Maybe things would have turned out differently."

"What do you mean?"

"We found the severed hand of a man named Bob Sommers. Apparently he was also from San Diego and was an acquaintance of your missing person, Katherine Ramirez."

"You had a homicide… here?"

"Two, actually."

"Two? And they are tied in to Kate Ramirez. How?"

"Our first victim, Robert Sommers was last seen

with this man." The chief showed Mary a coroner's picture of Tony. "Do you know him?"

"No. Who is he?"

"We don't know. His ID doesn't match his prints. Sure you haven't seen him?"

Mary thought about it. He did look familiar. "I don't know him, but I think I saw him at The Sands. That's where I followed Kate to from the airport. She's staying in room 202. This guy was sitting smoking a cigar on a bench in the courtyard looking at Kate's room."

"That's interesting. Is there anything else you can recall about the guy?"

Mary thought about it. "No, sorry."

"Who knows, maybe he was sent here to find your missing person. Do you want to tag along to search John Doe's hotel room and see if we can figure out who he is and why he's here? I'm on my way there now."

"Yes, thank you. Absolutely."

"First time to Kauai, Ms. Valentine?"

"Yeah."

"Well, at least this way you can see some of the sights."

Mary smiled and said, "Are you this nice to all visiting assistant prosecutors?"

"Of course."

"How many have come to see you?"

"You're the only one," the chief said with a smile.

CHAPTER 36

When Kate and Amy finally got to the dirt parking lot for boaters, Vina was standing there waiting for them with the boat's owner.

"I'm so sorry we're late. If I told you why, you'd never believe me," Kate said, having finally settled on keeping Tony's death a secret, at least for the time being. After introductions and brief chit-chat, Kate handed over the cash and signed some documents on the hood of the Jeep. The two women, whose paths had crossed for similar reasons, hugged and wished each other well with their respective journeys.

After unloading the provisions into the dinghy, Kate pulled Vina aside. "Remember the guy you said was in the front office at the Inn? Well, he somehow found me and followed me from The Sands to the grocery store. I thought I lost him but he switched cars and tried to run us off the road over by the lighthouse."

"Is he still following you?" Vina said as she looked around.

"Um, I don't think so. But be careful when you drive the Jeep, Vina."

"You think he'll try and follow me?"

"I doubt it, but be careful anyway. Here are the

keys. The pink slip is in the glove box." Vina tried to give Kate an envelope with cash, but she refused to take it. "The Jeep is yours. You've been a great friend, Vina. I don't know what I would have done without you."

"But I'm the one who led that guy right to you," Vina whispered.

"It's not your fault."

They hugged, and Kate left Vina standing next to the Jeep. Vina yelled out, "Hey, which boat is yours?"

Kate used her hand to shield the sun and pointed. "The sailboat with the blue hull anchored closest to shore."

"*Nani nui*. The name means 'big and beautiful'," Vina added.

"I'm gonna run Amy and the coolers out to the boat first and come back for our bags and the other stuff. Can you keep an eye on the luggage for a few minutes?"

"No problem," Vina said.

They dragged the bags onto the sand and Vina sat down beside them. Once the dinghy was launched, Kate looked back and held up five fingers to Vina to indicate it she would only be a few minutes. The outboard engine cranked right up, and Kate went full throttle out to her new boat.

❋ ❋ ❋

A moment later, Manuel walked up and sat in the sand beside Vina. "You know those two?" he asked.

Vina took a long look at Manuel and replied, "I don't know, do you?"

"As a matter of fact, I do know one of them. What I don't know is where they are sailing off to."

"That's too bad," Vina said sarcastically.

"Not really, because you're gonna tell me where they're heading."

"I am?"

"Yeah, you are," Manuel said as he shoved a gun into her ribs. "We can do this the hard way, or the *very* hard way. The choice is yours." Vina froze. She couldn't speak. She had no way of knowing Manuel was holding a pellet gun purchased from Wal-Mart. For all she knew this crazy guy was going to shoot her in the side right then and there, and the thought terrified her. "Okay then," Manuel continued. "I'll choose for you. Let's do this the hard way. The very hard way means I kill you right here and now. I'd rather not do that. So what you're going do is stand up very slowly and walk with me to that red Jeep over there."

Vina was paralyzed by fear and couldn't move, so Manuel grabbed her by the arm and pulled her to her feet, the gun still pressed against her ribs. He helped her into the passenger seat and grabbed the roll of duct tape he'd left on top of the tire. He quickly and expertly bound her wrists together in her lap and taped her ankles as well. Vina looked around for someone she knew, but the only people nearby were tourists. The town of Hanalei was just around the corner; maybe she could yell for help when they passed through. But that idea quickly faded when a strip of tape was fastened over her mouth.

Ultimately, Manuel avoided passing through town

by using the Jeep's four-wheel drive to hug the shore of the Hanalei River until coming to a dirt road that led up into the mountains. It didn't take long to end up in the middle of nowhere, and Manuel stopped the Jeep next to one of the power-line poles that skirted the dirt road. Once the engine was off, there was only silence, except for the muffled pleas coming from Vina. Manuel shoved the weapon in his waistband and ripped the tape off her mouth, not caring if she screamed because there was nobody around to hear. And that was a good thing, because during the drive up the mountain Vina had gone from petrified to pissed off.

"What is your problem?" Vina yelled.

"Well, since you asked, I need to know where Kate and her little friend are going and I need to know right now."

"I don't know where they're going, so this was all a waste of time."

"Oh, I don't think so. It looked to me like you and Kate were pretty chummy back there. I'm guessing you know exactly where she's planning to take that fancy new boat of hers. I'm also guessing you're going to tell me what I need to know."

"Guess again," Vina said defiantly.

Feeling he was losing the upper hand, Manuel punched her in the stomach, hard. The blow caused Vina to crumple and fall out of the Jeep to the ground where she curled up in a fetal position. She'd never experienced pain like this before. She was gasping for a breath and then she vomited in the dirt. She would have cried, if she had air in her lungs to do so.

"Why don't you think about my question a little longer?" he said. Manuel didn't want the interrogation to drag on too long because he wasn't sure when Kate was going to set sail, and he wanted to be there when she did. Manuel had been a United States Marine and served in Iraq. He could break a man's spirit in under an hour and get all the information he needed, mostly without killing anyone. Torture was a powerful tool to get a person to talk. Out here there was no Geneva Convention to prevent him from doing whatever he liked. "Alright," he continued, "maybe the first question was too hard. Let's start with something simple. What's your name?"

Vina didn't say anything. Instead she remained in a ball on the ground. The first punch felt like it had torn a hole in her midsection. Whatever he did, she wanted to make sure she didn't get hit there again. Manuel grabbed her by the hair, yanking her to her feet.

"Didn't anyone tell you it's rude to look away when someone is talking to you?" Manuel dragged Vina to one of the power poles. "From now on, you are going to look me in the eye when I talk to you." Manuel used the tape to secure Vina to the wood pole in a standing position. "Don't go anywhere," he said before laughing at his own joke.

Manuel searched the Jeep for anything that could connect him to the girl, just in case he was pulled over on his way back. He found her purse and pulled out her driver's license and read her name and address aloud.

"Well, hello, Vina Kealoha, of 121 Omao Road, Hanapepe Heights." He zipped her license at her like a

Frisbee, hitting her in the face. "Now I know where your family lives. Don't think I won't go straight there and kill them all if you don't tell me what I need to know."

Three generations of her family lived in their Hanapepe Heights home. She said a silent prayer for Kate as she made the decision to tell this psycho whatever he wanted to know.

Manuel continued scouring the Jeep, tossing this and that aside until he came across a slip of paper in the glove box. It was a note, in what looked like a woman's handwriting, on stationery from The Sands. It read:

Departing: July 18th
From: Hanalei Bay
To: Lahaina, Maui
Boat: Sailboat, Hunter 33

The name "Amy" was scribbled in the top corner. Manuel brought the note over to Vina, who clearly didn't look well and was possibly bleeding internally from the blow.

"Don't die on me yet, Vina," Manuel said as he slapped her hard to bring her back to the moment. He held the note up to her face and asked, "Do you know who wrote this?" Vina took a good long look at the note.

"Yes," she said. Now maybe the beating would stop.

"Who is Amy?"

"It's Kate's sister from the mainland."

"Kate has a sister? I didn't know that."

"It's her stepsister. The one she left with back on the beach," Vina said as another wave of nausea overcame her and she hurled again.

Manuel ignored her. "Hmmmm." Manuel put the note in his shirt pocket and reached into his shorts and pulled out the gun. It was all for show, but he wanted to be sure she kept her mouth shut in case she survived.

Vina couldn't take her eyes off the gun. "No! Please, just leave me alone. Please."

"I don't know. I don't like leaving loose ends."

"I swear, I won't tell a soul what happened. Don't kill me. Please."

"It doesn't look like this is your day," Manuel said as he pointed the gun at her. Vina closed her eyes and braced for the bullet. "Alright, against my better judgment, I'm going to leave you out here to die rather than put a bullet in your brain. Just remember, when you die of dehydration, it was your choice." She nodded in capitulation. Manuel went to the Jeep. "Okay, have it your way," Manuel he called out as he started the engine. Spitting dirt from the tires, he did a donut turn and headed back down the mountain.

Vina let out a sigh of relief until she realized she was taped to a pole, miles from anywhere.

CHAPTER 37

The closer the dinghy got to the boat the more excited Amy became. The boat was beautiful. They came along-side and Kate hopped off, helping Amy aboard before securing the dinghy.

"Okay, I'll start handing you the coolers if you'll stow them below," Kate said.

Amy didn't say anything but was looking around the boat at the instruments and ropes, wondering how it all worked. Amy slowly put the coolers on the bench seat, clearly lost in thought. "Does this boat have a motor?" she asked.

"This boat has a diesel engine, but around here we really won't need it. There's plenty of wind."

"Good to know," Amy said as she started to take the coolers below.

Kate looked around and said, "Okay, everything is below deck. Can you organize it? Put the perishables in the fridge and the rest can stay in the coolers or put it away. I'll go back and get the luggage."

"I got it."

"Are you going be okay here alone?"

"Yeah, I'll be fine."

"Okay then. When I get back I'll give you the grand

tour and show you how everything works. Until then, it may be best if you don't touch anything that looks important," Kate said, not waiting for a reply. She started the dinghy's outboard engine and sped off back to the beach.

Amy went below and began opening each drawer and inspecting every nook and cranny of the boat. What she was looking for she wasn't sure, but she'd know it when she saw it. After a thorough search of the boat, she found a few interesting items, but nothing helpful. It was sweltering down there, so she went topside and started looking under each seat cushion, and that's when she found what she wanted. In a waterproof case was a handgun. Amy pulled the gun out, a Springfield 9MM, and released the clip. It was empty. Dammit. She searched high and low for the ammo but could not locate even one bullet. Amy then heard the dinghy approaching and put the gun back where she found it, just before Kate boarded, all smiles.

"Is this a beautiful boat or what?" Kate said.

"It's nice."

"Here, help me get the luggage on the boat and I'll secure the dinghy. Want to hear something weird? Vina took off and left our luggage on the beach."

"Maybe she had somewhere she had to be."

"Maybe." Kate was concerned that Vina had gone, but she was more concerned about departing as soon as possible.

"You know what all this stuff is and how it works?" Amy asked as she looked around at the sailboat's rigging.

"Yeah, I know how to sail," Kate replied, even though a lot of what she knew came from books. This trip would be the true test of her seamanship.

"I'm glad at least one of us knows how to work all this stuff," Amy added.

"I'll teach you as we go. Don't worry. You'll do fine."

Kate adjusted the dinghy so they could tow it safely and walked around the boat smiling. "This is such a great boat. I can't believe it's mine."

"Mom said you had a big boat back home."

"That was Angel's boat. This one is mine. Have you looked around down below?"

"Yeah. It's really nice. So, where am I gonna sleep?"

"It's called the berth."

"Berth?"

"Sleeping quarters. I'd prefer to be close to the hatch in case I need to get topside in a hurry. So you can have the master stateroom, and I'll sleep back here," Kate said while storing the provisions.

"So what's the plan?" Amy asked.

"Get off this island as quickly as possible," Kate said. "The first thing I want to do is check the wind and weather." Kate set her guidebooks and charts on the table and plotted the first leg of their cruise into the GPS while she listened intently to the conditions on the VHF radio. There was a weather fax, which she didn't know how to work yet, though she wasn't worried. She had learned that summer was the best time to cruise the islands, even though strong trade winds could make crossing the channels dicey and make the windward sides of the islands less desirable to drop anchor for the night. Kate was relieved the radio weather report was calling for light and variable winds with uncharacteristically calm seas.

Amy came down below and asked, "Does this boat have a phone?"

"No, but she comes equipped with other ways to communicate with the outside world in case of an emergency."

"Is there some way for me to charge my cell?"

"Do you have a 12-volt adapter?"

"No."

"Then I'm afraid not. When we get to Lahaina we can hook up the shore power and you can charge it then. Who you gonna call anyway?"

Amy scanned the shore using the binoculars she'd found under the seat and said, "I'm not calling anyone. Just was thinking in case someone calls me." Amy saw a red Jeep driving along the road that hugged Hanalei Bay. She zoomed in and watched it pull off the road. A Hispanic man with a ponytail got out and scanned the water, looking at the boats.

CHAPTER 38

Mary and the chief were looking at a map of the island on the wall and discussing the case.

"Hey, Chief. Sorry to interrupt, but there's someone here you'll want to talk to," one of his officers announced.

"Who is it?"

"Vina Kealoha. She was carjacked at Wai' oli Beach Park."

"I'll be right there," the chief told his officer.

"Where's this beach located?" Mary asked.

The chief quickly found it on the wall map and said, "The beach is a dinghy landing for the boats anchored in the bay during the summer months. In the winter big surf makes it impossible to anchor there."

"Do you think this is related to my case?" asked Mary.

"Probably. We almost never have this kind of activity here. Let's go find out."

Vina was seated on a bench just outside the office. Clearly she had seen better days. "Vina, are you okay?" the chief said, resting a hand on her slender shoulder.

"I don't know. I guess I'm okay now," but the tears in her eyes told another story. She was clearly shaken.

"He warned me if I told anyone what happened he would kill my family. I believe him."

"What happened?"

Vina gave a detailed account of her ordeal while an officer took notes. She told them everything, including the fact that Kate Ramirez is alive. The man that grabbed her didn't think she would ever get away to tell anyone what happened. He also didn't know he took her up Powerline Trail, a semi-popular hiking trail. Fortunately, a group of hikers found her before nightfall and helped her get back down to the town of Hanalei.

"Is this the woman you know as Kate?" Mary asked as she showed her the picture from the jacket cover of her book.

"Yup. Except her hair is red now. Is she okay?"

"We don't know. Did the guy who kidnapped you tell you what the note said?" Mary asked.

"No."

"Did Kate tell you where she was heading?" the chief asked.

"I… I… I don't remember."

"What kind of boat did she buy?"

"That I do remember. It's a really nice looking sailboat with a blue hull."

"Do you know the make?"

"No, but I know the name," Vina said proudly. "It's called *The Great Escape*."

"Do you want me to alert the Coast Guard, Chief?" the officer asked.

"I'll take care of it," the chief said.

"Where do you think they're heading?" Mary

asked the chief.

"I'm just glad they're off my island. I mean enough is enough already. But if I had to guess, they're heading for Oahu."

"Why do you think they're heading for Oahu?"

"Well, unless they are heading for Tahiti, they have to be heading for Oahu. Other than the islands of Niihau and Lehua, which are privately owned and basically off limits to outsiders, Kauai is the northernmost island. The next island in the chain is Oahu. Take a look at the map and you'll see what I mean. My guess, Oahu is where they'll stop next."

"Kate told me they were going to Maui," Vina said as she began to pull herself together, though a little hesitant to contradict the chief.

He didn't reply but took another look at the map, running a finger along the path to Maui. "They would cross the Kauai Channel and hold a course for Pokai Bay and then fall off for Barber's Point. From Honolulu heading for Maui, they would have to cross the Kaiwi Channel, go around the south end of Lanai and then across to Lahaina."

"How long would that take?" Mary asked.

"Assuming the weather holds and they avoid all the possible pitfalls of the channel crossings, it would take a couple of days at least."

"Do you think the guy who kidnapped me could figure this all out, too?" Vina wanted to know.

"I don't know. Could you give us a good description of what he looks like?"

"It's a face I'll never forget as long as I live."

CHAPTER 39

Everything Kate read indicated it's much easier to sail between the islands at night, but she didn't want to chance it with a new boat and navigational equipment she wasn't completely comfortable with. Instead, she plotted a course for an anchorage a few miles away. Once Kate had the sails trimmed and the coordinates entered in the GPS, she was able to take the wheel from Amy and enjoy the ride. The boat sailed better than she imagined, easily cutting through the aquamarine water at a comfortable speed on a downwind run. Kate couldn't keep from smiling as she sailed her new boat in open water. Life didn't get any better than this. The island Kate had called home for the past few weeks was even more beautiful from this vantage point. There were white sand beaches set against deep green mountains with steep cliffs and waterfalls aplenty. A couple of miles into the cruise they passed Tunnels, the name for a popular snorkeling spot Kate had partially explored from the beach. The deeper outside of the shelf-like reef, where Kate had never gotten to, was now on the port side of the boat—it teemed with turtles and other exotic marine life. They could anchor here and swim around in the crystal-clear water for a while, but Kate wanted to be sure they got to their destination for the night before dusk.

"Amy, how about a beer?" Kate yelled to her stepsister who was down below, missing some of the most incredible scenery in the world.

Amy poked here head out and said, "What did you say?"

"I said, how about a beer? Get one for yourself and come up here and check this out. It's amazing."

"I'm unpacking right now."

"You can do that later. Now get some beers and get up here."

"Aye, aye captain," Amy said, saluting her stepsister. "Since when do you drink beer?" she asked while reaching in the fridge for two cold ones.

"Since I started to discover who I really am."

"And who is that?" Amy asked as she handed Kate a Heineken and plopped down next to her.

"I'm a simple girl who doesn't need to drink Martinis and have $200 lunches every day. I like burgers and beer."

"Come on, don't give me that. You've always liked the finer things in life—even when we were little. Remember the time you snuck out of our room to go out with Ricky Baldelli? You didn't even like him, but he was going to take you out to some fancy restaurant. He was like ten years older than you."

"I remember that night. He let me drive his red Camaro."

"Did you do him?"

"What? No way! I was, what, fifteen at the time."

"So nothing happened?"

"I didn't say that," Kate answered with a sheepish smile.

"That's what I thought."

"But you're right—I've always wanted a better life than what I had and I'd do almost anything to get it. And by a better life, I mean more expensive things. But I think I've finally figured out that the things I thought would make me happy really didn't."

"Well, speak for yourself. I'd like to live the good life for a while."

"Amy, look around—*this* is the good life."

❈ ❈ ❈

The anchorage Kate chose for the first night of their voyage was called Nualolo. It's a popular spot with the charter boats and snorkel tours. The good thing was, the boats were long gone at this time of the early evening and you were allowed to tie up to the mooring buoys for the night, as long as you left in the early morning. This was going to be a lot easier than trying to anchor somewhere with Amy at the helm. Kate steered the boat inside the reef to the buoy that offered the most protection. It took the two of them two tries to snag the line and secure the boat, but once they were hooked up, it was time to relax.

"Hey, I'm gonna go for a swim. Wanna join me?" Kate asked.

"Nah, you go. I'll start making dinner. How does a salad sound?"

"Yeah, good."

Kate spit into her mask and rubbed it around so it wouldn't fog up, then dove off the swim step into the warm water. The feeling of being alone in the open ocean should have been terrifying, but instead it was exhilarating. She felt a surge of adrenaline from the thought that this was her new life—sailing her own boat around the islands and taking early evening swims with Hawaii as a backdrop. She was so excited she thought she was going to burst.

❄ ❄ ❄

Back on the boat, Amy was again rummaging through Kate's things. Her search was more out of curiosity, but she was also looking for anything of value. To hide the fact she was foraging through Kate's clothes, she pretended to be unpacking and did put a few things away to cover her tracks. Amy knew Kate had always used a planner and was betting she'd brought one on the boat. Sure enough, there it was, tucked into the side pocket of a duffle bag. Amy opened it to the current date, and then worked backward. The planner served as a daily dairy, and right there in Kate's handwriting were two notations that made Amy both nervous and pissed. The first one read, "Found money Amy stole from me. Not sure what to do." The second entry read, "Get cash away from Amy and stash it in the bilge. Confront her when we get to Oahu. Use money to pay off the boat." Amy slammed the planner shut and checked to see if the cash was where she left it. It was. Now she had to find a place to hide it.

❊ ❊ ❊

The smell of hamburgers on the BBQ caught Kate's attention as she floated on her back a football field away from the boat. Kate was enjoying the setting sun as it glowed in the distance, painting the glassy water in reds and oranges.

"Are those hamburgers I smell?" Kate called out as Amy worked the grill attached to the railing.

"After what you said earlier, I figured hamburgers would be better than salad. Is that okay?"

The aroma of the hamburgers was impossible to resist and Kate swam back to the boat, pulling herself up on the swim step where Amy had set out a towel and a beer for her. Kate knew their water supply was limited, but indulged herself in a quick fresh water shower on the back of the boat and toweled dry.

"The burgers are almost done. Hungry?" Amy asked.

"Famished," Kate said.

"How's the water?"

"Oh my God, it's so nice. Tomorrow morning you have got to go for a swim," Kate said as she fumbled to turn on the boat's lights. "Can I help with the cooking?"

"Nah, I got it," Amy said, putting the buns on the grill, signaling it was almost time to eat. Amy played the part of the hostess in the hopes that she could get Kate to commit to giving her more money.

"I'm gonna go get changed. I'll be right back," Kate said and went below, wondering why Amy was being so nice.

❉ ❉ ❉

With a full belly, beer buzz, and everything stored and secured for the night, the two stepsisters sat and talked under a summer sky crammed with stars.

"How's Jenny doing, Amy?"

Amy wanted to scream, *Fine, no thanks to you!* Instead she said, "Jenny is incredible. She's really smart, you know."

"Good. What's her favorite subject at school?"

"English. Hey, maybe writing is in her blood, too. It's too bad she's stuck in such a crappy class. I wish I could send her to private school," Amy remarked, not realizing right away the implications.

Kate ignored the dig and asked, "Does she remember me?"

"No," was all Amy said as she drained the last of her beer.

"I'm so sorry I wasn't there for her—and you. I really am. You just don't know what it was like living with Angel."

Amy got up to pull two more beers from the fridge. "Pretty bad, huh? Couldn't have been any worse than living with my ex."

When Amy handed her the beer Kate said, "Look at this," and revealed the scar on her head where Angel ripped part of her scalp out, and some of the other dozen or so marks he had left on her.

"Oh yeah, look at this," Amy said as she showed Kate a big scar on the back of her thigh.

"How did that happen?"

"Bruce threw hot coffee on me when I got pissed that he was out all night and I asked him where he was the next morning."

"Is that when you left him?"

Amy hung her head and said, "No. That was when we first got together. I stayed with him another two years. I just stopped questioning him when he didn't come home—sometimes for days."

"What does Bruce do for a living?"

"He's in construction."

"I guess it doesn't matter whether your husband makes a lot of money or a little, a bully is a bully."

"You got that right, sister," Amy said and the two clinked their beers.

"How long did you stay with Angel after he hit you the first time?"

"Too long. At first he would feel so bad about it. He even cried. Man. He would feel so guilty about hitting me he'd try to make it up to me with cards, flowers, and gifts. Then little by little the apologies became fewer and farther between."

"Why didn't you divorce him and take him for all he was worth?"

"I wouldn't have gotten a dime. Believe it or not, Angel was broke. People think athletes have it made. Sure, they get a good salary. But they have to pay taxes. Then they have their accountants, agents, and managers, who all get a cut. There's also union dues and a bunch of other expenses. Add to that Angel was an idiot. He would give money he didn't have to his posse. People who only hung around him for the money. I don't know,

I guess I was partly to blame. I spent a lot of money on myself. But I felt I deserved it with all the crap I had to put up with. Plus there's the pressure to look like you're doing well because that's what everyone expects. I wish I would have taken some of Angel's money and invested it instead of blowing it."

"Did you put some money aside?" Amy asked, wondering where it was if any existed.

"Not really. When I finally got up the nerve to plan my escape I started scrimping and saving. Before that, I spent every dime I could get my hands on." Kate yawned. "I'm really tired. I think I'm gonna hit the hay. Thanks for making dinner and listening to me ramble. All that crap is in the past. I'm starting over—again. What about you?"

"What about me?"

"What are your plans when we get to Maui?" Kate asked.

"I don't know. I guess it depends on you."

"Me?"

"You said you would take care of me if I helped you. So…"

"I did say that." Kate pondered for a moment. "Let me think about it, and I'll figure something out."

"Why don't you just go back and get all the money from your book? You could still live here, but you'd be rich and famous."

"Not interested," Kate said, although the thought had certainly crossed her mind more than once. But her conclusion was always the same: Angel would almost surely sue her for defamation of character because of the book and then, true to his nature, he'd use that money to hire someone to beat her to death. She shuddered at the thought.

"That's pretty selfish, don't you think?" Amy countered.

"What are you talking about? If I go back, Angel will have me killed. Is that what you want?"

Amy didn't say anything at first, then muttered, "No, of course not." *That bitch*, she thought. *She's not going to give me shit. I knew it.*

"Amy, look, I'm really tired. Let's talk about it tomorrow, okay?"

"Yeah, tomorrow."

After Kate went to bed, Amy sat there thinking about all the ways she could get a bigger piece of the profits that were just waiting to be taken. She could sell the story of what Kate did and where she's hiding to a tabloid. That had to be worth something. She could go back to the agent and ask for more money. She could blackmail Kate for whatever cash she had stashed. Before Amy went to bed she was filled with hope of good things to come—for herself.

CHAPTER 40

"Jesus Christ!" Manuel yelled as he paddled the stolen dinghy around the boats moored in Hanalei Bay under the light of the moon and the Princeville Hotel on the hill. The boats were a lot farther out than it looked from land and he didn't want to start the small outboard engine and draw attention to himself. His arms were on fire from rowing and his level of frustration was growing. He didn't know dick about boats, but after this experience he knew he needed one with an engine. He also wanted a boat that wasn't occupied. He could "boat jack" one of the sailboats, but that would just complicate things. He didn't need any witnesses and he didn't want to have to kill anyone if he could help it. Kate had to die and so did the sister, but that was it. He wasn't going to kill anyone else—unless he had to. As a Marine, he'd killed during Desert Storm, but that was different. He wasn't going to go to jail for killing a bunch of Iraqis. Manuel had watched the two sisters leave the harbor under sail earlier but wanted to wait until nightfall to steal a boat. He figured he could make up the time if he could steal a faster powerboat. Besides, he knew where they were heading so he should be able to find them. His plan was to get ahead of them and play possum. He would kill the engines and act as if he were in distress. The girls would come over to help and "badda bing, badda boom," they would never be seen again. He'd sink their boat and that would be that. It all seemed so easy, until now.

Manuel rowed past a Grady White with twin 225-hp Yamaha outboard engines. This was exactly the kind of boat he was looking for. It was fast and should be easy to handle—even for a city dweller like him. As he paddled around the boat, Manuel made his decision. This was the boat he wanted. He had come to learn that a lot of the boats anchored in the bay were owned by people who either lived on other islands or elsewhere on Kauai, leaving them here for the summer, using them only on the weekends. He rapped on the hull with his oar waiting to see if anyone came up from below. Nothing. No lights were on and it appeared as if nobody was home. Manuel paddled to the back of the boat and carefully boarded the speedy sport fishing boat named *Reelin' In The Years*.

He opened the transom door and made his way to the controls. He checked the ignition—no key. Not that he expected it to be that easy. The cabin door had a padlock on it, meaning nobody was below, since the door was locked from the outside. So far, so good. Manuel searched around the controls for a key. He figured the owner of the boat was just as likely to hide a key as take it with him. If there was a key hidden, it would be somewhere near the controls. Sure enough, he felt under the seat and a key with a yellow float was hanging there. The key opened the lock to the cabin where the ignition keys were lying on the counter. Manuel wanted to get out of there as fast as he could, but he also didn't know exactly how to run this boat. He searched around for the owner's manual hoping for guidance. Fortunately, the owner of the boat was meticulous and highly organized. In addition to the owner's manual, the owner had laminated a checklist of what to do when starting and shutting down the boat. Manuel looked around for a knife and quickly found one with the fishing gear and went topside with the instructions, keys, and the knife.

He started the engines, cut the mooring line, and set off into the night. As he got the boat up onto plane, Manuel felt the rush of running a boat at night, as it cut easily through the chop. He switched on the running lights as soon as he was around the corner from the hotel. Once everything was illuminated, he checked the fuel gauge. It read full. Man, things were really going his way. Using the compass and depth gauge, he headed west in the direction Kate and her sister should have gone. After talking to a couple of boaters on the beach, Manuel had learned it was more than likely a sailing vessel heading down island would leave the bay and make a counterclockwise loop around Kauai, keeping the trade winds at its back. He'd also been told that many sailors make their channel crossings at night. Manuel hoped the girls were too green to try that and instead would anchor for the night somewhere on the northwest side of the island. His plan was to pass them and get into position to ambush them the following morning.

CHAPTER 41

When Kate awoke the next morning, the air was so still and quiet she could hear distant birds she couldn't see. With her coffee in hand, she took in the extraordinary scenery from the boat's swim step. It was quite hot already, but she was waiting for Amy to wake up so they could swim together. But after a while, she said, "Screw it," and jumped into the water, which was as clear and warm as a swimming pool—except this pool was filled with colorful fish. Kate treaded water a few feet from the boat watching the sun come up over the mountains to the east. She could have stayed in this position forever, but the snorkel tours would be here soon and she had to untie from the moorings. Besides, the thought of hundreds of tourists invading "her" private place wasn't a pleasant prospect. Kate swam back to begin preparations to set sail.

※ ※ ※

"What island is that?" Amy asked a short while later as they putted out of the anchorage using the sailboat's diesel engine.

Kate looked down at her map. "That's the east side

of Niihau."

"How much farther 'til we reach our next stop?"

"Amy, you're missing the point. Look around you. How beautiful is this? How about the flying fish we saw this morning and the rainbows over the mountains?"

Just then, a pod of Spinner Dolphins started leaping out of the water right off either side of the bow. "Amy, will you look at that? This is amazing!"

Amy just nodded her head and listened to the music playing, a reggae mix Kate had burned just for the sail. She had everything planned out down to what songs she would play and when. That was so Kate.

"Are you feeling okay?" Kate asked.

"I'm fine. I was hoping you could teach me more about sailing."

The seas were very calm, and the light wind meant Kate would have to be creative with the sails to get them going more than a couple of knots. "Okay. Here, take the helm. Keep this heading." Kate tapped the glass compass mounted just above the steering wheel.

"Where are you going?" Amy asked, excited and a little nervous at the same time.

"I'm going to set the sails and see if we can cut the engine and use the boat the way it was intended." Although it had been many years ago, Kate was quickly recalling all she had learned in her many sailing classes in San Diego's Mission Bay.

Amy took the wheel and did her best to keep the needle right on the mark. She would correct one way and then overcorrect the other. There were no other boats around and a lot of room to roam, but she still showed poor touch and technique.

Kate yelled down from the bow, "Amy, hold the boat steady. I don't want the boom to swing around and knock me overboard."

"What do you mean?" Amy asked.

"See this," Kate said as she tapped the boom at the bottom of the mainsail. "I don't want this to come around and hit me."

"What would cause it to do that?"

"If the boat turns hard or the wind suddenly shifts."

"Oh."

Kate climbed down, killed the engine, and started cranking the winch for the mainsail. It snapped to attention and the boat's speed hastened just a bit. Kate then set the jib to match.

"There, that's better," Kate said, quite proud of herself. "Isn't this glorious?"

"Yeah," Amy said as she forced a smile. "I'd rather be shopping in the city, but this doesn't suck."

"You're right, this doesn't suck. This doesn't suck at all." Kate was grinning from ear to ear as she moved about the boat checking this and that and taking in the scenery.

"Hey, you want some breakfast?" Kate asked.

"Yeah, I'm starving."

"Me, too. Just hold this course and I'll go below and scramble up some eggs."

"I didn't know you could cook."

"There's a lot you don't know about me, Amy. Heck, there's a lot I don't know about myself. That's why I'm so glad we're spending this time together. This trip will be the perfect time to catch up and patch things up. Do you want some more coffee?"

"Yeah, thanks."

Kate looked around to get her bearings and checked the compass before heading down to the galley.

A short time later, Amy yelled down, "Kate, come take a look at this."

"I'll be right there. I'm almost done here."

A couple minutes passed and then Kate came topside with two plates of scrambled eggs, bacon, and bagels. She set them down on the seat.

"What's up?" Kate asked as she glanced at the compass and checked the sails.

"See that boat over there," Amy said as she pointed to a speedboat out about a half-mile to port. "When I looked through the binoculars I thought I saw someone waving a shirt over his head. Shouldn't we go check it out or something?"

"Let me take a look," Kate said as she gazed through the binoculars. "I'll see if I can raise them on the radio." Several attempts yielded no response. "Either his radio isn't working or he doesn't have it on. I guess we better go check it out. Let me take the helm and you can eat your breakfast. It's right there," Kate said as she switched places.

"Thanks."

Kate began making the necessary adjustments to put their boat on a path with the distressed vessel. Once she had everything set, she wolfed down her food and prepared to pass the boat that drifted aimlessly in the light wind. Kate thought she'd pass by and ask the captain to turn on his radio so she could find out what was wrong. It looked like he was towing a dinghy so if worse came to worse, he had a way to save himself. Kate had Amy take the wheel while she lowered the sails and turned on the diesel engine. The boat would be a lot easier to handle under power than it would be with the sails up. As they approached, Kate took control of the boat and Amy looked through the binoculars. Even without the aid of the binoculars Kate could see that the boat had two outboard engines. It seemed strange that both engines would go bad. But it could happen—faulty gas (or no gas at all) or something electrical. Amy was transfixed as she stared at the boat but didn't say a word.

"Amy, what do you see?"

"It's just one guy and he's waving us over."

"Okay," Kate said as she spun the wheel to get even closer as they approached.

"Everything okay?" she yelled to the man. He shook his head.

"Does your radio work?" Kate asked.

He shook his head again.

"Do you want us to call for help?"

The man continued shaking his head and said he was going to get in his dinghy and come over.

Before Kate could object, he leapt over the transom and was pulling the starter cord to his little outboard engine. It made Kate wonder: If he had gas for the dinghy, why not transfer it to the main gas tank? Also, why didn't he drop anchor? The depth gauge read 50 feet. Surely a boat of that size and make would have an anchor and enough rope and chain to anchor at this depth. To just abandon your boat, an expensive boat at that, without securing it seemed odd. Instead of slowing down or stopping, Kate kept the engine in gear and went below. When she came back up, she had put on shorts and a shirt over her swimsuit and wedged the 9MM gun in the small of her back. Kate used the GPS system that came with the boat to enter the coordinates of this guy's boat and mark it—even though it was drifting aimlessly. It could come in handy later if someone wanted to try to save the boat. She also noted their current position and wrote it down.

"Hey, Kate," Amy said, "aren't you going to slow down or drop anchor or something? The guy in the dinghy can't catch up."

"I will in a minute," Kate said. The dilemma was what stopping—or not stopping—would mean. Kate weighed her options. She could keep going and call the Coast Guard, but that was problematic because not stopping to help a boater in distress was a major nautical no-no. He could report her based on her boat's name. Plus, calling the Coast Guard would mean she'd have to provide information about herself and the boat. And even if she picked him up, she should still call the Coast Guard.

"Kate, what are you doing? Stop!"

"Okay, I'm coming to a full stop," Kate said as she eased back on the throttle and left the boat in idle. No need to take a chance and turn it off in case they needed to get it started in a hurry. And she was still not sure what her next move was going to be.

"Are you okay?" Amy asked as the man approached in his dinghy.

"No! Why didn't you slow down back there?" he said gruffly.

"I wanted to get in deeper water before I stopped," Kate lied. "What's wrong with your boat?"

"I don't know. It just won't start," Manuel said as he hopped on board and tied his dinghy to the cleat next to the other tender.

"Do you want me to call someone to come try to get your boat going?"

"Nah, I just need a lift to the next town," Manuel said, all smiles now.

It was as if they picked up a hitchhiker on the side of the road, something two women driving alone on a deserted road would never do. Yet, here they were in the open ocean alone with a stranger, miles from civilization.

Amy quickly answered, "Sure, we can take you with us."

"I noticed you didn't drop anchor. Aren't you worried about your boat drifting?" Kate said rather matter of factly.

"Not really," was all the man offered.

"You want something to drink?" Amy asked.

"You got any beer?"

"Do we have any left, Kate?"

"No, we have water. I'll go get some," Kate said as she picked up the breakfast plates and went below to get the water. She didn't have a good feeling about this guy and had a hunch he wasn't the boat's owner.

Kate grabbed three waters and went topside. Kate heard Amy and the guy whispering but couldn't hear what was said. As she climbed the stairs the two abruptly stopped talking.

"Is everything okay? Amy?" Kate gave her a long look and handed her a bottle of water.

"Everything's fine," Amy said.

Kate kept eye contact with Amy as she introduced herself just to make sure she and her stepsister were on the same page. "I'm Kay, and you've already met Amy. What's your name?"

"Manuel," he said as he accepted the water, "My friends all call me Manny." He figured the less he lied, the less he had to remember later. Then again, he was going to kill them both so it didn't really matter what he told them. First he'd kill Kate and after having some fun with the other one, he'd kill her too.

"You look familiar," Kate said. "Where are you from?"

"Mexico, originally."

"Oh. What are you doing way out here?" Kate asked while taking a long swig of water. With very little wind, it was hot even this early in the morning.

"Fishing," was all Manuel said, even though he didn't appear to have any fishing gear on his boat.

Kate excused herself and went below to look at *U.S. Coast Pilot #7*, which has information on everything including harbors and channels. There was a small boat harbor nearby, but getting in and out looked a little sketchy. As much as she wanted this stranger off her boat as soon as possible, the best bet would be to drop him off at Port Allen. It was somewhat on their way.

When Kate came topside, Amy and the man were whispering again, which made her very uncomfortable. Her gut told her to get rid of this guy as soon as possible, but what could she do? The gun in her waistband wasn't loaded, and she doubted he would just hop in his dinghy and leave. But it was worth a try. "Uh, excuse me, you two. I can call for a tow and you can wait on your boat while we shadow you."

"I think I'd rather be dropped off at the next marina."

"Oh. Well, we can drop you off at Port Allen. Is that where you launched from?"

"No, but that Allen place will be fine. Thanks."

"Aren't you worried about your boat?" Kate asked again.

"Not really," Manuel answered.

"Do you know how to sail?" Kate asked their new and unwelcome cabin mate.

"Not really," Manuel said as he sat down and propped his feet up.

Kate started up the diesel engine and put the boat in gear. It was extremely calm this early in the morning and Kate figured the faster she could get to port, the better, so she decided against hauling up the sails, at least until the winds picked up.

"Is this your boat?" Manuel asked.

"I just bought it," Kate answered.

"You want to see the rest of the boat, Manny?" Amy asked, pulling him up by the hand.

"Sure," he said and followed her below.

Kate shook her head. Some things never change. She remembered that Amy could never go a week without sex. It didn't matter who it was, even a complete stranger. Kate decided then and there that she would also drop Amy off at Port Allen as well. She could keep the cash she had stolen. That would be her payment for going to New York and getting the money in the first place. Kate just hoped she would spend some of it on Jenny. There was enough there to get her into a private school. But she doubted the money would go toward tuition. What a shame that Jenny had a mother who regularly put her needs ahead of her daughter's.

After about fifteen minutes, alternating between being concerned for Amy and just letting her do her thing (to keep the guy away from Kate), Kate finally yelled down to the salon. "Amy, I need you come up here. The wind is picking up and I want raise the sails. I'll show you how."

Amy appeared from below, flushed and full of herself. "I'd rather steer the boat. You're better at the sailing stuff," she said.

Kate reluctantly agreed and went forward to haul up the main and then the jib sail. As she worked, Kate would glance back as Amy and Manuel switched from making out to simulated sex as they stood behind the wheel. Kate yelled instructions to Amy about how to position the boat as she worked the sails. When the boat suddenly shifted and the boom swung around, Kate didn't have time to duck as the metal slammed into her ribs and sent her flying into the deep blue water.

CHAPTER 42

"Have you ever been in a helicopter?" the chief asked Mary as they waited to lift off.

"Are you kidding? I've barely been in airplanes," Mary admitted. "You think we'll be able to spot Kate's boat from the air?"

"It's worth a try. You can't have enough eyes out here looking."

"Is the Coast Guard still going to conduct a search?"

"They'll keep an eye out on their normal patrols and monitor the radio for any chatter, but no, they aren't going to go out of their way to look for someone who bought a boat and is sailing around the islands. When you think about it, she's not in distress and she hasn't committed any crime."

"What about the kidnapping suspect?"

"Like I said, the Coast Guard will alert the tour boat operators to look for the boat on their normal routes, but honestly, they aren't going to be looking all that hard."

"So how did you get hold of a helicopter—and pay for the fuel?" Mary asked.

"You don't want to know," the chief replied.

"You two ready?" the pilot asked.

The chief gave a thumbs-up and Mary followed

his lead. The Hughes helicopter lifted off swiftly from the Hanapepe Port Allen Airport. In a matter of minutes they were airborne and Mary was staring at the most picturesque scenery she had ever seen. They quickly passed over the resorts and golf courses and gave way to a rugged beauty that was like a scene from a movie. The colors were so vivid and the landscape so breathtaking, Mary literally forgot to breathe. A strange thought crossed her mind. Here she was, up in a helicopter, flying over waterfalls and valleys, and it was a weekday—a workday. It felt a little like playing hooky, except this was work. What if she could make this her job? Her heart soared with the possibilities. Her eyes watered; she couldn't be sure if it was from the rush of wind as the helicopter banked or her epiphany about her potential new life here in the islands.

In her headphones, Hawaiian music serenaded her as she looked outside through where the doors had been removed in this open-air helicopter.

"Jack, do you mind?" the chief said to the pilot, gesturing to his own headphones.

"What? Oh, the music. Sorry, I'm so used to having tourists on board."

"I like it, and technically I could be a tourist," Mary said with a slight smile.

"Sorry, Mary, but you'll have to come back for a real tour. I'm trying to coordinate the search with some of my men. A couple of them agreed to take their boats out and search on their day off."

"Chief, you want me to stay on this course or do you want to do a grid search?"

The chief looked out the window and then at his map. "Stay on this course but drop down a little."

"You got it, Chief. Hang on."

The copter's nose dipped and they did a descent that made it feel like Mary's stomach was in her throat. They still had a panoramic view of the water, but the boats looked a lot clearer.

"Jack, stay on this heading until I tell you otherwise, okay?"

"It's your charter, Chief."

CHAPTER 43

Amy sat dejectedly on the settee, her hands and feet bound with duct tape while Manuel rummaged around below deck.

"What are you going to do?" Amy pleaded.

Manuel didn't respond and instead tossed the two women's luggage up from the salon. A brass ship's bell and other brass items followed.

"What are you doing, Manny? Are you stripping the boat to sell the brass?"

Manuel stuck his head up into the hatch and gave a look that meant, *get real*. He leaped up and headed for the bow where the anchor was stored and threw the anchor, chain, and line on the deck. Using a knife, he cut the anchor line in half and carried the anchor and chain back with him and set it at Amy's feet.

Amy began to panic as she realized what the implications of this move were. "No! No! This isn't what we agreed on. You said if I helped you get rid of Kate and made it look like an accident, we'd be partners. Partners!"

"When were you born?" Manuel asked her.

"What?"

"I said, when were you born?"

"1976."

"So you weren't born yesterday." Manuel smiled and continued his busywork.

"What are you talking about? You said…"

"I know what I said, but I changed my mind. Sorry."

"Sorry? Sorry? What are you gonna do?"

"What do you think?"

"I don't know. I don't know. I… I have a daughter. I have a daughter!"

"Yeah, well, I have a son, and I don't want him to have to go through life with a father who's in prison. So, I've got to tie up some loose ends."

"Okay, okay. You're going to use the anchor to get rid of the luggage and anything else that belongs to Kate. Now, that's smart."

While Manuel ran rope around Kate's luggage, he gave Amy the same look he did before—the "get real" look. Then he started running line around Amy's luggage, too.

"Wait, that's my luggage."

Manuel continued wrapping the anchor line around it.

"WAIT! Wait a minute. Don't throw that overboard!" she yelled.

Manuel wasn't listening so Amy decided it was time to tell him about the money.

"If you throw that bag overboard you are throwing away close to $20,000."

Manuel didn't even look up.

"Did you hear what I said? There's $20,000 in cash in there. Plus any money my sister had stashed away.

It's all yours if you'll let me go," Amy pleaded.

Manuel reached behind him and pulled out the familiar manila envelope bulging with $100 bills. "You mean this money?"

Amy hung her head and started to cry. "Please, I have a daughter. She's only seven. Oh, God, I don't want to die. Please."

Manuel grabbed the duct tape and ripped off a six-inch piece and put it over Amy's mouth without saying a word. He then started binding together the luggage, Amy, and the anchor. Amy started kicking and screaming, but the duct tape prevented her from moving much or making a sound. When Manuel was sure he had everything the way he wanted it, he picked up the crudely bound luggage and placed it on the swim step. Then he checked the lines connecting Amy to the luggage and hurled the anchor overboard. Amy watched in horror. The anchor sped through the deep blue water toward the bottom, pulling the line along with it. A second later, the luggage snapped from the swim step into the water and Amy knew what was next. And she cried before being pulled under the ocean to her death.

CHAPTER 44

It had been too long since Angel had heard from Manny, so he called the hitman from his throwaway cell phone. No answer. Angel had traded his autograph and the promise of more memorabilia to a deputy in exchange for getting his phone charged. Now he was able to call Manny every chance he got, but there was still no answer. Finally, Angel's phone buzzed in the middle of the night. He quickly answered.

"Where have you been? What's going on?" Angel hissed into the phone.

"I've been busy, okay. I've taken care of the problem once and for all."

Angel let out a long sigh of relief. "That's great, Manny. Thank you. I owe you."

"Yeah, you owe me, alright."

"Where are you now?"

"I'm sailing."

"What?"

"Relax, it's all under control."

"How did you do her?"

"Well, technically her sister did it."

"What do you mean her sister did it?"

"It's a long story, one I'll tell you when you give me

my money. The thing to focus on now is that fact that your problem has been solved."

"When will they find the body?"

"That could take a while. Just sit tight, and I think you'll be happy with the way things turn out."

"Sit tight? I've been sitting tight. I need to get out of here, clear my name, and get back to baseball before the season is over, which is only a couple of weeks away."

"I don't know what to tell you, Angel."

"Did you take pictures of Kate like I told you to?"

"Yup."

"Well, that proves that she was alive and that I couldn't have killed her—twice."

"Yeah."

"When can you get those pictures to me?"

"I already sent them to you."

"Sent them where?"

"To your house, man."

"You sent them to my house? You sent them to my house?"

"Where did you want me to send them?" Manuel asked.

"Not to my house."

"What are you so worried about?"

"Now there's a link between me and you and Hawaii. Think, Manuel."

"Well, what's done is done."

"Shit."

"Look, Angel, I've really gotta go. I'll contact you when I'm back on the mainland."

"Wait, wait."

Manuel had already hung up because the sailboat was taking on water fast. The holes he had hammered into the hull were working better than he expected and the sailboat was going down fast. Manuel made one last check to be sure everything that would float was stored inside the cabin so there wouldn't be a debris field left behind. He untied his dinghy, cranked up the little outboard and began to motor toward shore with $20,000 in his pocket and a plan to get the hell out of there.

CHAPTER 45

The minute Kate had hit the water she knew what she had to do—she'd been doing it for weeks now—she needed to play dead. If Amy and the man in the boat thought she was dead, they wouldn't come looking for her. Kate stared at the surface just a few feet over her head and tried to make what little air was left in her lungs last as long as she could. She counted the seconds, knowing what she had to do and she didn't want to wait a minute longer. She had to swim for the fishing boat that Manuel left behind. Kate ditched her shoes, shirt, and shorts under water. All she needed now was her bathing suit. The faster she could swim, the better her chance of survival. As the blackness of drowning started to creep into her consciousness, she slowly and carefully came to the surface. Looking around, she saw a sailboat—her sailboat—in the distance moving away from her. The powerboat she thought was somewhere nearby was nowhere to be found. If she didn't find the boat fast, she wouldn't make it. It was that simple. Kate didn't panic, although she had every reason to. Instead she used her heightened state to think more clearly. Taking into account the wind, currents, and landmarks she remembered from the charts, she started swimming in the general direction of where the boat should be. All those morning swims at Salt Pond Park had paid off. Kate felt good—for now—and was hopeful she could make it. Alternating strokes to conserve strength, Kate heard the sound of a helicopter off in the distance as she rested on her back, but couldn't quite see it yet. At this point she didn't want to be rescued. She wanted to write her own ending to this chapter in her life. So when the chopper got closer she dove down as deep as her ears could stand and waited for it to pass. This was either the bravest thing she had ever done, or the dumbest.

CHAPTER 46

Through the headphone mic, Mary yelled to the chief, "Did you see that?"

"What?"

"Over there. I think I spotted clothes floating in the water."

The chief told the pilot to turn the chopper around so they could get a closer look. At this point they were only a few hundred feet above the ocean. As they made a second pass, Mary spotted what looked like a shirt and shorts. "There. Right there."

"Got it. Mark the spot on the GPS."

"That's it?" Mary asked as the chopper hovered over the clothes for a couple of seconds and then banked left.

"Unless you want to jump in, there isn't much else we can do. I'll alert the Coast Guard, but it could be a while before they can get here," the chief said.

"Chief, we gotta go. We're running on fumes as it is," the pilot said as he headed the copter back the way they had come.

Mary sat back in her seat and wondered to herself, did Kate make it this far only to drown? Did someone push her in? Did her boat sink? It was too coincidental to find what looked like women's clothes floating in the ocean in the general area where Kate's boat should be.

"Mary, keep your eyes on the water. We may get lucky and find something else on the way in. You never know," the chief said optimistically.

Mary doubted it. Kate was likely dead—and Angel didn't do it. He couldn't have. It was time to rethink the charges against him. Her office could always bring charges at a later date, but she had to face facts. Kate was seen alive some 3,000 miles away from Angel—who was incarcerated at the time. There was enough reasonable doubt that even a first-year law student could get Angel acquitted. The weird part was, Mary didn't really care about "not getting her man" as much as she should. Was the fragrant tropical air making her soft? Mary looked out the window of the helicopter and wondered again what it would be like to live here. She could always find work as an attorney. Kate had given up everything to escape life on the mainland—because she had to. Mary wasn't as desperate, or was she? What would she be leaving behind? Waiting when she got home was a backlog of cases and a job that had taken over her life. There was her cramped condo, which had her deep in debt, filled with all her worldly possessions. There was no man to rush back for and unfortunately no prospects, either. Mary turned to the chief and asked, "Do you know of any job openings at the prosecutor's office here on Kauai?"

The chief smiled and said, "Did you bring your resume with you?"

CHAPTER 47

Swimming in the open ocean was a lot harder than doing laps in the protected waters of Salt Pond Park. Every few yards she would stop and float on her back, looking up the azure sky, watching the birds fly by. If she weren't pissed at herself for allowing Amy to knock her overboard, this would have been a nice experience. There was no way what her evil stepsister did was an accident. No way. How did she not see it coming? This could be the biggest blunder of her life.

When she heard a splashing sound near her feet, it occurred to her that her poor judgment could very well end her life. If you lived on Kauai long enough, you knew there were sharks in the waters off the north side of the island. Hell, there were sharks in the waters off the south, west, and east sides, too. Kate quietly rolled over and stuck her head under water to see if she could see caused the splash. There, circling below her was a shark, a big one. A surge of fear started to overwhelm her. She could hear the pounding of her heart in her ears. Kate tried to control her breathing and get her heart rate down. Sharks can sense fear and will see it as a sign of weakness—and attack. Kate also didn't want to start thrashing around, either. She stuck her head under water again and the shark was gone. Was that a good thing? The answer came quickly as the shark brushed by her and as it accelerated away Kate could feel the thrust from its powerful fin. Her heart rate was off the charts. This was not the way she thought her story would end. Kate kept her head under water and looked around in every direction. She didn't want to lose sight of the shark. When she came up for a breath, a sport-fishing boat was approaching. This was her only hope of survival, so she put her head down and started swimming as hard and fast as she could to put herself in the path of the boat. Her eyes burned from the salt water and her arms felt dead, but she managed to swim the 50 yards needed so she could be seen by the boat—or run over. Screaming and waving her arms, the boat sped by. Kate lost it. She started crying and couldn't stop. The shark could attack at any minute and there was nothing she could do.

"What in the hell are you doing way out here?" Came a voice from behind.

Kate looked behind her. The boat had circled back and was now idling right next to her.

"I ... fell... overboard... shark," she said managed to say, almost too exhausted and flustered to speak.

"Seriously? Grab this lifesaving ring and I'll pull you in," the captain of the big Bertram sport cruiser said as he made a perfect toss and landed the ring right in front of her. He wasted no time pulling her toward the boat and up onto the swim step, barking orders to a crewmember on the boat at the same time.

Someone wrapped a towel around her and helped

her up. Kate's arms and legs felt like jelly, and she pulled the towel tightly around her. She was shivering.

"You are one lucky lady," the captain said.

"You can get hypothermia even in this warm water," a woman added while rubbing her arms and shoulders to generate some heat.

"I… I… know. Tha, tha, thank you," Kate said through chattering teeth.

"I'm just glad we spotted you when we did. We also spotted a shark just a few feet away from you," the woman said.

"I… I…. know, it tried to k… k… kill me."

"That's what sharks do. I'm Captain Ron and this is my wife, Julie. What's your name, little lady?"

"K… K… Kate."

"Well, Kate, welcome aboard. We'll try to make you as comfortable as possible while we look for fish. I'll alert the Coast Guard about your boat, and we'll take you in with us as soon as we're done out here. I'm in the middle of a charter right now." Captain Ron pointed to his passengers, a group of three men rigging their gear.

"I'm j… j… just so glad I'm on this boat, I c… c… couldn't care less where we are h… heading," Kate replied.

"I'll tell you what, Kate," the captain said as he sat down next to Kate in on the transom of his boat, *Off The Hook*. "Technically, this is a fishing expedition, but maybe we'll also fish for your boat."

"I'd really appreciate that. Do you have to call the Coast Guard?"

"Uh, well, yes and no. I have to alert them; I just

don't have to do it right away. Why?"

"If we can find my boat, maybe there won't be any need to call the Coast Guard," Kate said, no longer shivering.

"I'm guessing there's more to this than meets the eye," Captain Ron said as he looked at his wife.

"It's a long story."

"I'm a really good listener. Honey," he said to his wife, "check on the guests and I'll be right there." She patted Kate on the shoulder and went to check on the charter group.

Kate told Captain Ron some of what had happened and he was right, he was a very good listener.

"Wow. That's quite a story. The first thing we should do is level with the guys on the charter. I'm sure they'd be happy to help you look for your boat. They're shahk bait anyway."

"Shark bait?"

"No, *shahk* bait. It means they are tourists with no real fishing skills."

"Oh."

"Come on, let's go. I'll introduce you to the guys."

The charter group peppered her with questions, curious about what happened, and Kate answered each one. They were impressed that she'd survived such an ordeal.

"I was hoping we could look for it while you guys fish," Kate said.

"What kind of boat is it?"

"A Grady-White."

"Really? Man, we gotta find that boat," one of them

said. "I've got a Trophy at home and Bill here has a Boston Whaler, but a Grady-White is the next boat we'll buy. Hey, Captain, I say we look for this lady's boat, okay?"

"That would be great. Thanks," Kate said.

Captain Ron told them they would troll while they searched. He gave Kate the thumbs-up sign and said, "We're on. Do you remember the coordinates from when you went overboard?"

"Kind of," Kate said as she gave Captain Ron what she thought might be the last location she saw the boat.

"I'm assuming it wasn't running when you went overboard or we wouldn't even be having this conversation."

"No, it wasn't running," Kate replied as Julie handed her a water.

"Was it anchored?" she asked.

"No."

"What the hell happened?"

Kate told her the rest of the story, covering everything and leaving no detail out.

"This would make for a good book," Julie said after hearing the whole story.

"I know. Believe me, I know," Kate rolled her eyes and replied.

"Do you think we could catch up to your sailboat?" Julie asked.

"I don't think so."

"Where was he heading?" Captain Ron wanted to know.

"The last time I saw my boat it was heading toward... Polihale?"

"Could be he's heading for Oahu. There are slips at Port Allen and Nawiliwili, but I'd bet he's heading farther south. It would be a lot easier to hide a boat there with all the marinas, especially the private ones in Makani Kau."

"We really should call the Coast Guard," Julie said.

"Let's wait a while," Captain Ron said to his wife.

Kate took in the information and decided Oahu was where she was heading next. It would be a lot easier to just go to shore with Captain Ron and his wife, catch a flight to Honolulu, rent a car, and start looking for her boat—and her stepsister. The problem was, everything she owned was on that sailboat—what little money she had along with her ID and credit card. Her other option was such a long shot it almost seemed silly. First, they had to find the stolen boat. Second, it had to have drifted away from the reefs and other water hazards and still be afloat. Then, she needed a lot of gas to get where she was going—and the keys to start the boat, assuming it was still in running order. Finally, she would probably have to navigate at night, with God knows what kind of equipment on board. If she were writing this for a book she would stop, delete the page, and start over. The problem was, there was no other way.

CHAPTER 48

Manuel kept checking to make sure the $20,000 was still in his pocket. He would collect his money from Angel when he got back to the mainland and start living large. He'd had his eye on a tricked-out Chevy Impala one of his homeys had restored and wanted to sell. He could pay cash for it, buy his longtime girlfriend some bling, and then take the boys to Vegas. Wait a minute, what was he thinking? He always said when he came into some serious cash he would buy a little beach cottage in Imperial Beach, a real fixer-upper, and spend his days working on it. He could flip it for a profit and then buy another and start building his real estate empire. He could stop killing and instead make a killing the old fashioned way—in real estate. Manuel started dreaming of his morning trips to Home Depot in the truck he would buy to get supplies for that day's work. That's when the little dinghy's engine sputtered and died.

"What the fuck?"

Manuel picked up the gas can and shook it. It was empty. He searched around for another can, knowing full well there was none—but he had to look. There were no oars, either.

Manuel stood up in the little boat and looked

around. He was off what looked like a huge deserted beach, but it was way too far away to swim in. Manuel was not a strong swimmer to begin with, and God knows what kind of creatures were waiting for him in the open ocean.

"Fuuuuuuuuuuuck!" he screamed at the top of his lungs.

How could he be so stupid and not bring along extra gas—or at least check what he had?

"Unfuckingbelieveable!" he yelled, followed by a tirade in Spanish.

Manuel took stock of what was in the little boat. No food and no water. Not good. There was also no anchor and to make matters worse, the boat was drifting away from the shore—and fast. Things were going from bad to worse. He had no idea where he was. His plan was to put some distance between himself and the sinking boat and then go ashore. What he hadn't counted on was the fact that this side of the island was almost uninhabited and there was no place to put ashore safely. He assumed there would be a marina he could pull into and ditch the dinghy. He could then hitch a ride into town and get off this island before anyone figured out what had happened to Kate and her sister. So far, everything had gone as he planned and he knew that things would work themselves out. Worst-case scenario, he would drift to the island in the distance. He didn't know which island it was, but there had to be an airport there. Wait a minute. Manuel tried to remember what Kate was saying about the next island over. What was it called, again? Oh well, it was part of Hawaii, so he was sure there was someone there to help him. He had cash and cash was king, even here in the islands. Manuel decided to relax and enjoy the ride not realizing the island in the distance would not welcome him or his cash with open arms.

CHAPTER 49

It didn't take long for Captain Ron to locate the Grady-White. He knew these waters like only a local fisherman with over 30 years of experience could, plus he had all the latest and greatest electronics on his big Bertram to make finding a needle in a haystack more than probable. The boat had drifted out into open water and was right were Captain Ron said it would be, given the wind and currents. The crew secured the boats together and Kate thanked everyone for helping, then pulled Captain Ron aside and asked him, if she were to look for her sailboat, where would she start? The two of them poured over the charts and Captain Ron gave Kate a rough idea of where her boat was most likely located, based on several assumptions. Once Kate was aboard the stolen boat, she started the two outboard engines and checked everything out. When she was underway, she hailed Ron on the radio frequency he'd instructed her to use and told him her heading as she searched for her sailboat. She was then going to return the Grady-White to its rightful owner. It was the least she could do. Captain Ron insisted that Kate stay in radio contact just to be sure she made it back safely. With a wave, Captain Ron and Julie powered off in search of fish while Kate went on a fishing expedition of her own. Using one of the charts from below, Kate began her search by following the path that would likely lead to the location of her boat—and the two people who tried to kill her.

※ ※ ※

Manuel was baking in the sun. The only shelter from the intense rays was his shirt, which he was now using as a makeshift hat and sun protector for his face. Manuel heard the sound of a boat approaching and quickly sat up and removed the shirt from his face. In the distance, a bunch of charter boats hugged the coast—big catamarans, it looked like—but it was hard to tell from where Manuel was now. Off in the distance a powerboat was heading in his direction. *Thank God*, he'd be saved. He was dying for a drink of water and to get out of the sun. He started calculating what he would be willing to pay for a ride back to shore. He scooped the envelope with the $20,000 off the bottom of the boat and shoved it down his shorts. Along with the money, Manuel also saved Kate's wallet to prove to Angel that he had indeed killed her. He would explain to whomever passed by that his boat sank and he's been drifting out here ever since. This was true. He was a victim. The more he thought about it, the more he realized he shouldn't have to pay a dime to get a ride back to port. The boat drew closer. Manuel stood and waved his arms, making sure he was seen. The boat neared but slowed down a few hundred yards away and came to a complete stop a minute later. Manuel strained to see, but he was staring straight into the sun and the boat was too far away to really get a good look.

※ ※ ※

Kate stopped the boat a good distance away from the man alone in the dinghy. She had approached two other boats and done the same thing. She wasn't going to get too close until she was sure. Kate took a long look through high-powered binoculars and a smile formed in the corners of her mouth. "Gotcha," she said as she made her way toward Manuel. Kate thought about trying to reach Captain Ron on the radio and tell him where she was and that she found the scum who'd stolen her boat, but she decided against it. She could also call the Coast Guard and report the piracy, but she wanted to first find out what happened to her sister and her boat—and she hoped to be able to not have to explain who she was and what she was doing with a stolen boat. Instead, she would proceed with extreme caution and make sure this time she wasn't the one left for dead in the middle of the Kauai channel.

Kate approached at full speed so Manuel wouldn't have time to figure out what was going on until she was right on top of him. She passed Manuel in the dinghy at full throttle, throwing a large wake his way. This was to get him off balance and to make sure he didn't try and fire off a shot at her. Kate didn't know whether he had a gun or not, but it was better not to take any chances. As Manuel and the dinghy rocked violently, she pulled up alongside.

"Don't I know you from somewhere?" she yelled over the noise of the engines. "Now put your hands up over your head so I see them."

Manuel did as he was told. He stared at Kate, shocked and pissed she was still alive. There went his big payday. He scanned the horizon and there was nobody around for miles. The best way out of this was to tell the truth and hope she would let her guard down so he could make his move and kill her—again.

"You look like you've seen a ghost, Manuel, or whatever your name is," Kate yelled.

"Hey, you got me. What can I say?"

"For starters, what's your real name and where are you from?"

"Manuel's my real name, and I'm from Chula Vista, near San Diego."

"I know where it is! Do you know my husband, Angel Ramirez?"

"Yeah, I know Angel. Why do you think I'm here?"

"Angel sent you to find me?"

"To kill you." Kate just stared at him in disbelief. "Okay, at first it was just to find you, then Angel offered me more money if I could make you and your stepsister disappear." Manuel admitted this as if he was shot up with truth serum.

"What happened to Amy?" Kate asked, working the throttles to keep from drifting too close.

Manuel shrugged and said, "She's probably sailing your boat to another island by herself," bending the truth to fit his inherent goal.

Kate let that sink in. Could Amy sail herself to safety? Would this guy let her? The answer to both questions was no.

"I don't believe you," Kate yelled as she idled the boat close to the dinghy, but still a safe distance away.

"I don't know what to tell you," Manuel said with a smile.

"What happened? How did you end up out here?" Kate asked.

"What do you mean? Amy wanted to sail your boat to Maui. I wanted to get back to the mainland as fast as possible to collect my money from Angel. So I took the dinghy and headed back to Kauai, but I ran out of gas," Manuel said, picking up a gas can and shaking it for effect.

"Keep your hands where I can see them," Kate reminded him. "You're lying, Manuel. My sister couldn't sail to save her life, and you know that. She would never make it to Maui on her own, and I doubt she would try."

"She's your sister."

Kate pondered the situation and said, "Well, then I'm going to go look for Amy. Sorry, Manuel, but you're on your own. Good luck."

Kate started to power up the engines and speed off but Manuel stopped her when he yelled out, "Okay, she's dead. Your sister is dead! Are you happy?"

"Amy died? How?"

"Well, after she tried to kill you by knocking you overboard—which I had nothing to do with, I'll have you know—she pulled a gun on me and threatened to throw *me* overboard. I had no choice."

"Manuel, you're lying, again. I had the gun when

I went overboard. Nice try. So you killed my little sister, why?"

Manuel looked at her and said, "Look, I want to tell the truth, but we have to come to some sort of agreement, first."

"Manuel, what can you possibly do that would make me believe you?" Kate said as she used the twin outboards to maneuver the Grady-White to within shouting distance, but far enough away so Manuel wouldn't do anything stupid, like try to light a gas can on fire and throw it at her.

"Hear me out, okay?"

"You don't seem to be in a position of power, Manuel." Kate was enjoying this, channeling years of anger that still festered inside her. "What I should do is puncture your rubber dinghy with this gaff and sink it so you'll know what it feels like to be stranded in the middle of the open ocean. I'm guessing you wouldn't last long, so you'd also get to find out what it's like to drown."

"Now come on!" he shouted

"No, you come on. I'm going to give you one chance to tell me why I shouldn't sink your dinghy or just leave you stranded out here."

"First of all, I have something of yours that you're probably going to want back."

"What's that?"

"Your wallet."

"Okay, I'm listening."

"As a show of good faith, in exchange for your wallet I would really like a bottle of water," Manuel said, trying not to sound as desperate as he felt.

"Deal. Throw my wallet to me and I'll get you some water," Kate agreed.

Manuel took the wallet out and threw it to Kate. It landed in the middle of the boat. Kate used her foot to drag the wallet close enough for to her to pick up, all the while keeping a close watch on Manuel. Kate reached into the boat's built-in cooler and grabbed two waters and tossed them to Manuel, who proceeded to chug them both without a word.

"Man, I needed that. You got another water in there?" Manuel asked.

"Maybe. First, I want to know what happened to Amy. I mean really happened to her."

"We need to do that *quid pro quo* thing again before I tell the truth," Manuel said with a smile.

"What do you want?"

"What do you think I want? I want a ride back to shore."

"If you tell me what really happened to my stepsister, my boat, and everything you know about Angel, I'll tow you in to Nawiliwili."

"Nawiliwili? Is that some kind of joke? What about that Port Allen place?"

"No, we're past it already. Besides, Nawiliwili is the harbor where the cruise ships dock and it's only five minutes from the airport. Do we have a deal?"

"Fine. What do you want to know?"

"Let's start with something easy. Where's my boat?"

"It sank."

"You sunk my boat? Jesus Christ. I spent every-thing I had on that boat."

"I'll tell you what, you forget that I ever set foot on your boat and you can have half of what's inside this envelope."

Kate looked at the fat envelope, the one filled with the money Amy had stolen and stashed in her bag—her money.

"Deal," Kate said. Manuel took two stacks of bills out, then waved Kate over so he could toss the money in the envelope into her boat, which he did.

"So what really happened?" Kate asked.

Thinking that he was winning Kate over and it was only a matter of time before she would let her guard down and he could kill her, he felt no qualms about tell-ing her the truth—at least his version of the truth. "Your stepsister is dead. I'm sorry."

"Did you kill her?"

"Of course not."

"So how did she die?"

"She tried to shoot me with a flair gun. After she knocked you overboard, she got greedy. She wanted it all. She said she had a will that named her as beneficiary to all of the money from your book. She was afraid I would ruin her plans by exposing her as a murderer or blackmail her, so she tried to kill me. She shot the flair gun at me but it missed and went down into the boat and started a fire. I took the dinghy and got the hell out of there," Manuel said, impressed by his ability to spin a story like that off the top of his head. Maybe he would become a writer, too.

"So you left Amy to burn with the boat."

"Better her than me."

Kate shook her head. She didn't believe Manuel's version of events, but she didn't doubt that Amy was dead and her new boat was at the bottom of the ocean—and that Manuel was directly responsible for both. However, she wanted to know more, so she played along.

"I guess I should be grateful," Kate said. "She did try to kill me, too. Tell me more about your arrangement with my husband." She threw another water over to Manuel and turned off the engines to preserve gas, keeping a safe distance by using a gaff to push off.

"Well, he called me from jail and asked me to find you so that he could prove he wasn't a murderer. Then, when your book became a best seller, he saw his chance to not only clear his name, but to get rich, too. He figured if you died over here they would have to release him and he would get all the proceeds from the book."

"That bastard. So he told you to kill me and make it look like an accident?"

"Yup."

"And how much did he offer to pay you for killing me?"

"A hundred grand. Now that the cat's out of the bag, I'd be willing to tell all of this under oath, for a fee, of course," Manuel said, safe in the knowledge Angel would never be in court because Kate wasn't going to make it back to shore alive.

"How much?"

"Same as Angel offered—$100,000—and I'll tell the court how your husband hired me to kill you. Since you're not dead, I'm not guilty of anything."

"How can I be sure you won't change your mind about testifying when we get back to San Diego?"

"Throw me a pen and some paper and I'll put it in writing," Manuel said.

"I'll tell you what—you write out exactly what Angel told you to do and how you stole my boat and pass it back to me and we have a deal."

"Fine. Pass me a pen and some paper and I'll put it in writing."

Kate started the engines again and got closer so she could throw a pen and some pages from the ship's log to Manuel. He took ten minutes to write everything down and then wadded up the paper up and threw it back. Kate read what Manuel wrote and gave him a thumbs-up. "This is perfect. Thanks."

"So, how far is it to the harbor you talked about?"

"It's on the other side of island. You might as well make yourself comfortable and take a nap. It's gonna take a while to get there," Kate said, throwing a towline to Manuel.

"Wouldn't it be better to leave the dinghy here and ride in together?" Manuel suggested as if he were an innocent bystander in all of this.

"Tie this line to the bow of your boat, and I'll tow you in. I'd feel a lot safer this way. Make sure to secure the rope so it's good and tight. I don't want to lose you on the way, you being my star witness and all." Manuel grunted and tied some kind of crazy knot in the nylon line. He made another plea to ride back in the fishing boat, but Kate told him to just sit tight.

"Come on, Kate. I'm not gonna do anything now. You have my word."

Kate tried not to laugh, so she just kept her head down and worked on fastening the painter line to the Grady-White.

"You ready?" Kate asked as she took up the slack by giving the boat a little gas.

"Do I have a choice?"

Kate expertly throttled up and settled on a speed that made for a smooth ride for Manuel in the dinghy. She looked back and gave him the thumbs-up sign, which he returned as he sat on the bench seat facing forward. Kate motored along following the contour of the coast for a mile or so before she gradually veered off into deeper water. She heard Manuel yell from behind her.

"Hey, Kate, you're going the wrong way. KATE! What are you doing? We had a deal!"

Kate just ignored him and towed him farther and farther out to sea. She checked the gas gauge—the boat was either burning very little fuel, or had huge tanks. Either way, she didn't have to worry about getting back safe. Manuel, on the other hand, was going to be miles from anywhere when she was done with him.

"You bitch! I'm going to kill you just like I did your sister! You're dead, you hear me? DEAD!" Manuel yelled something further in Spanish as he tried to untie the knot that held the two boats together, but was getting nowhere because of the tension the towing caused. Kate made sure Manuel's next port of call would be somewhere in the Marshall Islands some 1,200 miles away. All she had to do was put him in the right spot and let the currents do the rest. Kate ignored Manuel's name-calling for another 45 minutes before she reduced power.

"Manuel, it looks like this is as far as I can take you." Kate cut the towline with a knife. "Have a nice life. I know I will. *Adios, amigo*," Kate said over the screaming of Manuel, who looked like he was getting ready to jump in and try to swim to her boat. Kate didn't stick around to find out—she sped off toward the island of Kauai.

❊ ❊ ❊

Kate found Port Allen on the GPS and plotted a course there. She seriously thought about going back for Manuel and towing him in. Despite what happened to the fat guy back chasing her up the cliff, she wasn't a murderer. Leaving Manuel out here to die felt an awful lot like murder. She tried to rationalize it a number of different ways, but the guilt she was feeling about setting someone adrift miles from land with no provisions made her extremely uncomfortable. Would he make it to land or be rescued at sea somehow? She doubted it. His chances of survival were pretty slim. But her chances of survival if she let him live were just as bad. Could she live with her decision to leave him out there alone? The answer surprised her: yes, she could. Sure, she could have turned him in to the local authorities, but he would weasel his way out and kill her. No, it had to be this way. This is how the sequel to her first book had to end. The heroine rides off into the sunset—and that's just what Kate did. Making it into the harbor just as the sun set in the west.

❋ ❋ ❋

After securing the Grady-White in an empty slip at Port Allen, Kate went to the Harbor Master's office to drop off the keys along with a note about what happened. Returning the boat to its rightful owner was only the first of many things she had to set straight. Then she used the pay phone to call the Kauai Police. She would confess to killing the big hairy man chasing her and report that her stepsister was likely lost at sea—and she would sign both reports using her real name.

"Chief, you are not going to believe this," an officer said with his hand over the phone. "There is a Kate Ramirez on line 1 who wants to report a missing person and tell us about our John Doe."

"Put her through," the chief said.

"Uh, hi, my name is Kate Ramirez and I want to—"

"Oh, I know who you are," the chief interjected, his pen at the ready. "What I want to know is where you are."

"I'm calling from a pay phone near the showers at Port Allen Harbor, why?" Kate asked.

"Because there is someone who is dying to meet you," the chief said, immediately regretting his choice of words.

"Really, who?" Kate said, ignoring the word choice.

"A woman from the prosecutor's office in San Diego who followed you all the way here regarding your husband's case."

"Yeah, I'd really like to clear that all up. Is she still on Kauai?" Kate asked as she dropped the last of her quarters from her wallet into the pay phone.

"She sure is. In fact, she's standing right next to me. Do you want to talk to her while I send someone to come get you?" the chief asked.

"Yes."

"Mrs. Ramirez?" Mary asked while the chief sent someone down to the docks to get the elusive author.

"Yes. Who am I speaking to?" Kate asked.

"I'm Mary Valentine. I'm the Deputy District Attorney in San Diego assigned to your case."

"What do you mean my case?"

"We've been holding your husband for murder. You were the, um, victim. Obviously, we will be dropping those charges against him, but I was wondering if you wanted to press charges against him for other offenses?"

"Actually, I have a signed confession from a man that my husband sent to Kauai to kill me. Isn't that attempted murder?"

"Probably, and we can add that to the felonious assault and hopefully other charges, if you're willing to proceed with this," Mary said.

"You can count on it," Kate said firmly.

"Excellent," Mary said, smiling. "And Kate?"

"Yeah?"

"I really loved your book. It's changed my life."

Kate laughed and said, "Thank you so much. I guess you could say it's changed my life, too." Kate smiled at the experience of her first fan encounter. It felt good. "It just goes to show, truth is stranger than fiction."

"I don't know. Your novel was a pretty wild ride."

"Ms. Valentine, you have no idea what I have been through in real life. It's too bizarre to be believable."

"You can call me Mary. And yes, I'm anxious to see how it all ends."

"Me, too," Kate said.

After the conversation, she sat down on a bench to watch all the charter boats returning from their sunset cruises. The truth was, Kate had been working on the perfect ending ever since this ordeal started. The problem was, real life endings aren't always as neat and tidy as a novel and sometimes a happy ending isn't possible. She worried about who would look after her niece now that Amy was gone. Her stepmother, probably but she knew Jenny's father was a lot like Angel and the thought of him getting custody of her was frightening. Kate decided she would do whatever should could for Jenny, even if it meant becoming her legal guardian. Speaking of legal matters, the first thing she would do when she got back to California was divorce Angel—and try to bankrupt him in the process. Another legal issue she had to deal with was straightening things out with her publisher to get back every penny owed to her from her literary agent. Last, but not least she had to decide where to live and what to do with the rest of her life.

EPILOGUE: ONE YEAR LATER

"Jenny, come in here, it's going to start any minute," Kate yelled down from the balcony of her sprawling Princeville estate on Kauai to her niece, who was out front playing with a friend. Even though her place was nicer than anything she'd lived in with Angel, it felt honest. Her life had an authenticity now that her life in San Diego never had. She'd truly earned this and, better yet, had enough left over to regularly donate a significant percentage of her income to a national non-profit that helped victims of domestic violence.

"We're coming, Aunt Kate," Jenny yelled back. She then turned to her friend, who was also staying on the island for the summer, and said, "My aunt is going to be on TV tonight. It's kind of a big deal. She's been freaking out all week. Let's go see what all the fuss is about."

"Come on, come on. Sit down, you two. You're just in time," Kate said, patting the big couch in front of the giant plasma TV. The room was a large, open-air space with vaulted ceilings and a view of the ocean.

The sound of the ticking clock signaled that *60 Minutes* was back on and Leslie Stahl introduced the segment: "The path to becoming a best-selling author is never an easy one, but novelist Kate Ramirez is probably the first writer who had to kill herself just to get on the *New York Times* Best Seller List—and lived to talk about it."

"Is that true?" Jenny's friend asked.

"You'll see. Just watch" Kate said, realizing how important this interview was to her.

"We went to the island of Kauai to catch up with the reclusive author to find out how fact and fiction blurred when Kate Ramirez disappeared from San Diego two years ago to escape her abusive husband, professional baseball player Angel Ramirez. She wound up with a best-selling book and a brand-new life in the process." The screen filled with an aerial shot of the posh resort community of Princeville with Hanalei Bay in the background. "This is where Kate Ramirez lives today, but less than a year ago she was on the run, hiding out in a little cottage on the other side of Kauai, working as a hostess trying to put her past behind her," Stahl narrated as they showed footage of the Plantation Inn and the Westside Brewing Company.

"What made you run?" Stahl asked Kate on camera. "I mean, you were married to a famous baseball player living the life of luxury and you traded all that in for a simple life on the dry and dusty side of a tiny island," Leslie Stahl asked Kate on camera.

"I had no choice. If I stayed with my husband, I'd be dead by now. I know there are women out there watching this who will understand when I say I was more afraid to leave my husband than I was of staying with him, even after all the years of physical and emotional abuse. When we were first married—actually before our wedding now that I think about it—Angel would belittle me. He made me feel like I was an idiot. When I would accuse him of cheating on me—which he was—he'd make me believe I was crazy and paranoid just to think it. I guess I felt like I deserved to be treated like this, that somehow I was to blame. The first time he hit me I was shocked. The second time I was angry. By the tenth time he beat me I was used to it. I know how crazy that sounds, but after a while you get to a point you really believe you are worthless. To escape my sad reality I started writing. It was my salvation. I created this character that was stronger and braver than I was. Through my character I was able to do things I wasn't able to do in real life."

"Like leave your husband," Stahl interjected.

"Yes. Through my writing I realized there was a way out. I wanted my character to create a new identity and come up with the cash to vanish without a trace. As I researched how to do it and started writing it all down, I began to believe I could do it for real. Of course it took me a while to get the courage to actually do it. It also took me a long time to get the money to disappear. I discovered Angel had put us deep in debt and forged my signature on loan documents and credit card applications I didn't even know existed. He didn't even bother to make one payment on any of these, so my credit was shot. Then I finally had proof Angel was seeing someone else and I confronted him. He beat me so badly he broke my ribs and knocked me unconscious. I'd finally reached my breaking point."

"Yes, but you left behind a book that had all the

clues for anyone to find you. Did you secretly want to be found?"

"God, no. I had no idea my book would be published, let alone become a best seller. In hindsight, it was a big mistake to have submitted my manuscript to an agent. I just forgot all about it. But I can see how all the media attention surrounding my 'murder' would make my book an interesting read."

"Did you ever intend for your husband to go to jail for killing you?" Stahl asked.

"Of course not. I just wanted to get away from him and I chose a place that was remote enough where I thought he wouldn't be able to find me. The problem was, it was so remote that I didn't watch the news or read a newspaper for weeks, so I had no idea what was going on back home."

"Your husband is now in prison after being convicted on lesser charges, isn't he?"

"Yes, but unfortunately, he is eligible for parole in less than ten years."

"He still scares you, doesn't he?"

"Of course, but in a different way than before I left him. He doesn't have the same power over me he once did, but the fact remains, he sent someone to kill me— and he nearly did. That's scary."

"What happened to the hit man that Angel sent after you?"

"Leslie, you'll have to read the sequel to find out." The real Kate and the Kate on the TV screen both let out a slight smile simultaneously.

"That's right. You've written a follow-up to your

first book, *Angel*. What's this new one called?"

"*Devil*. It's a continuation of the first book. And as life seems to imitate art, at least for me, anyway, my character learns a lot about herself and finds an inner strength and independence she didn't know she had. Of course there is a lot of action and adventure, too. Most of the best parts of the new book I didn't even have to make up—I lived them."

"What did you think of a movie being based on your first book?"

"I'm excited. It looks so far like it'll be really good. I've been on the set a few times—it's not far away—and it's hard to believe my book will be a movie."

A clip from the movie was shown. Kate's character is speeding along in a red Jeep through the dirt roads of Kauai with a big dog by her side, and a pickup truck is in hot pursuit. Of course this never happened, but like her book, a little creative license goes a long way.

Leslie Stahl then narrates over footage of Kate walking on the beach near her house and in the guest cottage behind her estate that she converted to a writing retreat.

"So life is good?" Leslie asks Kate.

"You know what? Life *is* good. And it's not because of the fame or the money. What makes me happy is who I became because of my ordeal. In the past I think I thought of myself as a victim, and that's exactly what I became. Today, I feel like I deserve good things to happen to me and they are. I won't lie to you, Leslie. I am living out my dream. I love my life. I just want people to know that no matter what happens, or happened to them, they should never lose hope and never give up going after their dreams, whatever they are."

＊ ＊ ＊

As soon as the segment ended, the phone rang. "Hello?"

"So, how was it?" It was Carol, the former assistant to literary agent Sandi Golding. She sounded very eager. "I wasn't able to catch it when it came on here—I had to DVR it. But I can't wait to hear how it went."

"Well, they didn't drag my name through the mud, thank God. Oh, and they mentioned the new book," Kate announced proudly.

"I'll call McGunne at Gladstone and tell him. I know he'll be happy. I wonder if our friend is watching from wherever the hell she is," Carol said, referring to her former boss, who had taken a page from Kate's book and disappeared without a trace. Following Sandi's disappearance, Carol immediately started her own literary agency and retained almost every one of Sandi's clients, including Kate.

"In a way, I wouldn't be where I am without that bitch," Kate said and started laughing.

"Yeah, but she ruined a lot of people along the way," Carol said sadly, "including, literally, Tony Gravano and Bob Sommers."

"I know, I know. It's weird, though, how dying a tragic death can be a career booster."

"You mean because Gravano's book became a bestseller and Sommers' CD is now a cult classic?"

"Exactly. I just hope Angel doesn't decide to write a book," Kate said sarcastically.

"Speaking of Angel, did you hear that his libel and defamation suit was thrown out of court yesterday?" Carol asked.

"Yeah, Mary told me."

"Who?"

"Mary Valentine, the prosecutor from San Diego on Angel's criminal case. She moved over here when she was done with the trial."

"Oh, right," Carol said. "I saw her on some of the morning shows when that was all going on."

"Yep. And you'll definitely want to check out her manuscript when it's done."

Just then the doorbell rang and the girls screamed, "We got it."

Mary and Vina walked through the door with a bottle of wine and a beautiful lei. "We're here to celebrate your newfound national celebrity," Mary said, looking fit and fabulous in a sundress and sandals. She was adapting quite well to island life.

"Yeah, great interview," Vina added, putting the lei around Kate's neck.

"Speak of the devil. Mary's here and so is Vina," Kate said into the phone.

"Vina?" Carol asked.

"My friend from the Plantation Inn. Did you read my manuscript or just send it straight to the publisher?"

"No, of course I read it. But I thought you'd changed the names. Vina is a real person?"

"Yep," Kate replied. "Vina is very real, and she's

pouring me a glass of wine as we speak."

"Okay, I'll let you go. I'll call you after I watch the interview tomorrow."

"Carol, you work too much. It's Sunday, for God's sake. Hell, it's early Monday morning there. Go out and have some fun tomorrow!" Kate admired and smelled her lei. "I'm sure having fun. In fact, I just got leid."

"What did you say?"

"Nothing."

"Okay, I'll talk to you later," Carol said.

Kate hung up and told Mary it had been Carol on the call.

"I hope she works on my book," Mary said.

"Me, too," Vina added, who now assisted Mary in the Kauai prosecutor's office while studying to become a lawyer herself. "Then, maybe Mary won't pile so much work on my desk."

"Here's to our success, then," Kate said as they clinked their wine glasses in a toast.

Kate looked out the window at Jenny and her friend chasing the golden labrador Kate had bought from Kimo. The two kids rolled around with the puppy on the expansive lawn, laughing loudly.

"How's she doing?" Mary asked, nodding toward Jenny.

"There are good days and bad days. I know she misses her mom, but her grandmother has stepped in and is raising her right. I'm paying for her to go to one of the best private schools on the east coast, and I come and visit whenever I can."

"It must be nice having her here for the whole

summer," Vina said.

"She's an angel," Kate said.

"I never thought I'd hear you say 'angel' in a positive way again," Mary said.

"Well, as long as those royalty checks keep coming in for *Angel*, and the other Angel is behind bars, I'll be able to say it with a smile."

ABOUT THE AUTHOR

This is Lee Silber's first novel, but he has spent a lifetime preparing to write it. Silber is a water enthusiast who enjoys surfing, sailing, and scuba diving. For nearly two decades, he has spent a part of each year in Hawaii. He is also an accomplished musician and avid baseball fan. He, his wife and two sons live in Mission Beach, California. In addition to writing books, Silber keeps a busy schedule of speaking engagements, corporate training, and consulting, helping creative people become better at the business side of the arts and business people to be more creative. In 2012, he spent a week on Kauai photographing many of the places featured in this book. To get your free companion guide, go to www.LeeSilber. com. Silber is the award-winning author of 18 other books, including a popular series of business books for creative types featuring *Organizing From The Right Side Of The Brain*. His last three releases include *The Wild Idea Club*, *No Brown M&Ms*, and *Bored Games*.

MAHALO

In Hawaiian, the word for thank-you is *mahalo*. I'd like to say mahalo to my wife and friends for listening to me ramble about characters and plots until the wee hours of the morning. *Mahalo nui loa* (thank you very much) to my agent, Toni Lopopolo, who has skillfully guided my writing career for 15 years and several books—and is nothing like the fictional agent in this book. *Aloha* to Andrew Chapman, my publishing and literary consultant, who wondered why I had to actually go to Hawaii to research and write this book—and why he wasn't invited. If it weren't for Andrew and all of his help, this book wouldn't exist. A big mahalo goes to my mom for reading and reviewing all 19 of my books. Finally, mahalo for the incredible support and encouragement from the fans of my other books—especially those who took the time to send fan mail. The idea for this book was conceived on Kauai. It would not be possible if it weren't for such an inspiring place.

Made in the USA
San Bernardino, CA
16 December 2012